**"Luke, you d[...]
this job jus[...]**

"Just to maneuver you into my bed, Gemma?" Luke taunted. "Not entirely, but I won't deny it was one of the deciding factors."

"But..." Gemma shook her head, shocked at Luke's unmasked desire.

"But what? But a man with my background shouldn't aspire to such heights. Is that what you're trying to tell me, Gemma? That I'm not good enough to go to bed with?"

"Luke, you don't mean this," she protested. "You don't want me. You wouldn't even like..."

"What I'd like, lady, is to roll you on your back and make love to you until the only sounds coming from that soft mouth of yours are moans of pleasure."

Gemma shivered. It would be so easy to indulge in the pleasures Luke described—so easy to ignore his womanizing reputation.

PENNY JORDAN was constantly in trouble in school because of her inability to stop daydreaming—especially during French lessons. In her teens she was an avid romance reader, although it didn't occur to her to try writing one herself until she was older. "My first half-dozen attempts ended up ingloriously," she remembers, "but I persevered, and one manuscript was finished." She plucked up the courage to send it to a publisher, convinced her book would be rejected. It wasn't, and the rest is history! Penny is married and lives in Cheshire.

Books by Penny Jordan

Don't miss any of our special offers. Write to us at the following address for information on our newest releases.

Harlequin Reader Service
901 Fuhrmann Blvd., P.O. Box 1397, Buffalo, NY 14240
Canadian address: P.O. Box 603,
Fort Erie, Ont. L2A 5X3

PENNY JORDAN

JORDAN

an expert teacher

Harlequin Books

TORONTO • NEW YORK • LONDON
AMSTERDAM • PARIS • SYDNEY • HAMBURG
STOCKHOLM • ATHENS • TOKYO • MILAN

Harlequin Presents first edition March 1989
ISBN 0-373-11153-3

Original hardcover edition published in 1987
by Mills & Boon Limited

CHAPTER ONE

'DARLING, it's so good to have you home. You can't imagine how much there is to do! Sophy's aunt hasn't the faintest idea of how to go about organising a large wedding, and so she's left absolutely everything to me.'

As always, implicit in her mother's welcome was the message that her love was conditional upon Gemma's performance in her unwanted role as daughter of the house. All through her years at boarding school and then later at college Gemma had heard that dual message. At one time she had even been hurt by it, wishing that her mother wanted her home purely because she loved and needed her. But with maturity had come the wisdom to accept her parents as they were.

It was not entirely her mother's fault that she held all real emotion at bay; first her parents and then her husband, Gemma's father, had actively encouraged her to be the pretty, silly, dependent woman she was.

In an era that encouraged women to think and live for themselves, her mother was something of an anachronism, Gemma recognised. At one time, just as she had ached for her mother's love, so she had also ached to see her assert herself as a human being, but now she could recognise what she had not been able to see then. Her mother had worked too hard and too long at being the wife her father wanted her to be to change now.

Her father did not want an independent woman as his wife, he did not want her mother to be able to meet him on his own level; he preferred to treat her as a pretty, dim-witted child, and Gemma had long ago recognised that that was their pattern of living and that to change it would mean that their relationship would end. It was when she had seen the futility of fighting against the feminine mould her parents wanted to cast her in that she herself had left home. She was not like her mother; *she* could never settle for the life her mother had led, always the inferior partner in a relationship that was totally opposed to everything that Gemma believed the relationship between a man and a woman should be.

She knew that both her parents were disappointed in her, in their different ways. Her mother had wanted her to be a carbon copy of herself: a daughter who would grow up to enjoy her love of shopping and lunches with her women friends; a daughter who would marry early, have two children, and make her home within easy reach of her parents.

Her father had wanted very much the same thing, with one qualification. First and foremost he had wanted her to be her 'daddy's girl' and he had been prepared to pay for the privilege with expensive presents and spoiling.

Gemma had learned enough about life and human nature now to feel saddened and sorry by the narrowness of her parents' lives and perceptions.

Other people viewed them differently, of course. Her father was an extremely successful businessman, and her parents were among the most wealthy inhabitants of the small Cheshire village where they lived.

David, her brother, was one of the directors of her father's building company. Unlike her, he seemed quite happy to fit into the mould their parents had designed for him.

Now David was getting married and it was his wedding that had brought her home. Luckily the date of the wedding fell right in the middle of her school's long summer holidays, so there had been no problem about her giving in to her mother's plea that she return to Marwich to help with the preparations for the big day.

She hadn't been surprised to learn that her mother was organising everything. No doubt her father had had a hand in that decision somewhere. She could just see him now, his rather austere face creased into a faint frown as he stood in front of the fireplace in his study, hands clasped behind his back in his favourite Prince Philip pose, whilst he suggested to David that it might be as well if their mother handled all the arrangements for the wedding.

She wondered rather wryly what Sophy Cadenham had thought of that decision. Gemma didn't know her brother's fiancée very well; for one thing Sophy was only twenty-one to her own twenty-five and, for another, both she and Sophy had spent all their teenage years away at their respective boarding schools. Sophy's schooling had been paid for by one of her more well-to-do relatives. Although an orphan, Sophy was what Gemma's mother described rather snobbishly as 'extremely well connected', which meant, Gemma reflected rather ruefully, that she was a cousin, once or twice removed, to the Lord Lieutenant of the County.

Both Gemma's parents were pleased about the match, and Sophy's aunt, a rather thin, tired-looking woman who had been widowed just about the same time that Sophy lost her parents, and who lived just outside the

village in a pretty grace and favour house of Queen Anne
origin, owned by 'Sophy's cousin, the Lord Lieutenant', had apparently been more than delighted to hand
over total responsibility for organising the wedding to
Gemma's mother.

Despite her rather vague and 'helpless little me' airs,
Gemma's mother was a skilled organiser. Their house,
the largest in the village with its extensive grounds,
would make a perfect setting for a June wedding. The
date had been decided when David and Sophy announced their engagement at Christmas, and now, with
the big event only a week away, the hired gardeners were
working tirelessly to bring the lawns and flowers to
perfection.

A huge marquee was going to be erected in the
grounds; Sophy's wedding dress, which had come from
the Emanuels, was hanging upstairs in one of the guest
room wardrobes, and the Lord Lieutenant and his lady
had deigned to accept their invitation. In fact, the Lord
Lieutenant had actually agreed to give Sophy away,
much to her mother-in-law-to-be's delight.

The last thing her mother really wanted was her help,
Gemma recognised, remembering ruefully down
through the years how often she had heard the same
plaintive sound in her mother's voice, and how often her
childish heart had leapt with delight at the thought of
being able to help her.

It had taken her a long time to learn that her mother
did not really want her help; that she didn't want
anything from her, in fact, other than her pretty
obedience. To her mother she was a toy to be shown off
and paraded before her friends, not a human being at all.
Just as David had been brought up as the son of the

house, his father's heir, a proper manly little boy, so she had been brought up as a shy, pretty little girl.

Only she had broken free of that confining image to make her own life.

She came out of her reverie to hear her mother saying her name rather sharply.

'Gemma, you were miles away. I was telling you about the guest list. I want you to go through it for me, and help me with the table plan. The place cards will all have to be written out, too, by hand—typing them is so common.' She made a face, a pretty moue, that grated on Gemma, although she didn't let her feelings show.

'You're looking so tired, darling.' He mother's concern held a faint edge of bitterness. 'Daddy and I can't understand why you insist on working at that dreadful place. Daddy could have got you a job much closer to home at a far nicer school.' She gave a tiny shudder of distaste. 'Some of those dreadful children you teach aren't even clean.'

Compressing her mouth against her mother's distaste, Gemma wondered what on earth her parents would say if she told them that she would ten times rather be with her unclean, ill-educated pupils than here in her parents' luxurious home.

Long ago she had decided that she wanted to teach; that had been something that was always there. Her desire to teach those who most needed the benefits that education could give, and who were least likely to receive them, had come later, growing gradually, and so far she had no regrets at all about her choice of career.

Of course there were heartaches and problems; days at a time when she ached for the sight of green fields and trees; weeks and months when she battled unsuccessfully against the oppressive weights of poverty and suspicion; nights when she lay awake, aching beyond sleep for the hopelessly narrow and deprived lives of her pupils. For some of them, from the moment they were born, the odds were stacked against them. It was her job, her private crusade, to offset those odds. When she had first arrived at the grey, depressed inner-city school the other teachers had warned her that she would soon lose her bright optimism, that she would be victimised and even physically abused by some of the children. She had been told she was too young and too pretty to teach the adolescent boys, many of whom could and did try to harass their female teachers. But even after three years of enduring all that Bower Street Comprehensive could throw at her she still held true to her original ideals. If she managed to open the gate that, via education, led to an escape from the grimness of his or her life for only one child, then she had achieved something.

This inner need to help and encourage these children wasn't something Gemma had ever discussed with anyone else. The other girls at the university with her hadn't shared her views on teaching, and her colleagues were often as ground down by the harshness of their surroundings, and the pressure of living in an area where so few of their pupils would ever be able to get even the most menial of jobs, as the pupils and their parents were.

'Gemma, you aren't listening to a word I'm saying.'

Gemma looked up and saw that her mother was frowning at her. How different this pretty, floral sitting-room was to her own grim flat. This room was her mother's alone. It had french windows opening out on to a York stone-paved patio with tubs of flowers, beyond which stretched lawns, and trees. Her father had designed and built this house twenty years ago, with the proceeds from his first successful contract.

Since Christmas the whole house had been redecorated and refurbished in readiness for the wedding, Gemma thought wryly. Her mother's sitting-room, which she had last seen decorated in soft creams and pinks, was now all delicate yellows and french blues. A pretty floral fabric of a type often featured in glossy magazines hung at the windows and covered the plump settee. A huge bowl of yellow roses filled the marble fireplace, and the antique sofa table that her father had bought for her mother several years ago was covered in silver-framed photographs of the family. The entire ambience of the room was subtly expensive, faintly 'county', and Gemma stifled a faint sigh as she looked through the windows to the gardens beyond.

She missed this view more than she ever wanted to admit; she missed breathing clean, fresh air, and looking out on to green fields and tall trees. She knew that it wasn't possible for all people to be equal, and she also knew that her father had worked extremely hard to get where he was today. She didn't think it was wrong that her parents should have so much while others had so little, but she did think it was criminal that they should be so little aware, so little caring, of the reality of how other people lived.

Her mother had been shocked and disgusted on the only occasion she had visited her daughter in her small north Manchester flat, Gemma remembered. She had hated the narrow mean street, and the towering blocks of council flats; she had done everything she could to persuade Gemma to get another job, to come home and allow her father to use his influence to find her something more suitable, more acceptable to their friends, perhaps teaching small children at the local village school. Her father's company had a contract to build an extension on the local comprehensive and they had also given generously to the appeal to raise money for a swimming pool for the school, she was sure that . . .

Gemma had cut her off there. She didn't want to change her job, but trying to explain that, and to explain why, to her mother, had just been impossible.

'David and Sophy have gone round to the house. It really is lovely, Gemma. You *must* go and see it. Your father had it built for them as a wedding present. It's just a nice size for a young couple: four bedrooms and a pretty nursery suite. I do hope they won't wait too long before starting a family . . .'

Gemma let her mother chatter on as she tried to suppress her own growing feeling of alienation and tiredness.

'Of course your father had to invite him, but I was hoping that he wouldn't accept the invitation. He's not really one of our set, and if it wasn't for the fact that he and your father do business together, I wouldn't invite him here at all. It's amazing that he's done so well, when you think how he started, but I must confess that I never feel comfortable with him. The problem is that since he isn't married, where are we going to seat him?

'Businesswise, his company is now much bigger than your father's, and your father won't want to offend him, but he's hardly the sort of man one could put on the same table as the Lord Lieutenant, is he?'

Gemma frowned. 'I'm sorry, Mum, I missed half of that. Who are we talking about?'

'Oh, Gemma! Luke O'Rourke, of course.'

Luke O'Rourke. Gemma felt the room sway crazily round her, and she gripped hold of the chair back in front of her while her mother carried on, oblivious of her shock.

'Good heavens, you haven't met him yet, have you? I'd forgotten that. He was away at Christmas—I think he went to the Caribbean or somewhere on business— but you must have heard me mention him? He owns O'Rourke Construction—they practically built most of the latest stretch of motorway network round here. I'm not really quite sure how he and your father met, but over the last couple of years they've worked on several ventures together—those apartments your father's building in Spain, and the extension to the school. Luke is based in Chester.'

Gemma let her mother rattle on. Luke O'Rourke. It couldn't be the same man, surely? It had been stupid of her to be so shaken just because of the familiarity of the name. Luke O'Rourke. She closed her eyes unsteadily and then opened them again. It had all been so long ago. Over ten years ago now. She had been what . . . fourteen, almost fifteen? She shook her head, trying to dispel the images crowding her mind while her mother busily sought a way of dealing with the problem of where to seat Luke O'Rourke.

She could always seat him with Gemma, of course. Although she hated admitting it even to herself, Susan Parish found her daughter disturbing. Why on earth couldn't Gemma be more like the daughters of her friends, content to marry a nice young man and settle down to be a wife and mother? And if she *had* to work, to teach, *why* did she have to work in that awful school with those dreadful children, half of whom couldn't even speak English? Whenever Gemma was around she was always on tenterhooks, terrified that she would upset her father, or make one of her dreadful sarcastic remarks. She wouldn't put it past Gemma to say something upsetting or controversial to the Lord Lieutenant, and she had been racking her brains for a way to avoid having the two of them together on the top table. As Sophy's closest male relative it was of course quite acceptable for him to be there, and even though Gemma had refused to be a bridesmaid, it would still have looked odd to have excluded her from the intimate family group. Now, though, she had the perfect excuse. Luke O'Rourke was definitely not 'family' but, as a 'close friend and her husband's business partner', it would be perfectly acceptable to pair him with Gemma, especially since she was not participating in the wedding as a bridesmaid. Breathing a tiny sigh of relief, Susan Parish went back to her mental arrangements, leaving Gemma totally unaware of what was going through her mind.

In the hall the grandfather clock chimed the hour. 'Oh, my goodness, I promised the vicar I'd see him this afternoon to discuss the final arrangements. Would you like to come with me, darling, or will you be all right here?'

The last thing Gemma felt like doing was joining her mother. Summoning a diplomatic smile, she shook her head.

'I'm afraid I'm feeling rather tired. Would you mind if I stayed here?'

Relieved, Susan Parish patted her hand. 'Of course not, darling. You *are* on holiday, after all. Oh, by the way, did I tell you that Daddy is bringing some people back for dinner tonight? Wear something pretty, won't you? You know how much Daddy likes to show off his pretty little girl.'

Only by the strongest effort of will was Gemma able to prevent herself from saying that she was neither pretty nor little. She didn't want to upset her mother, who would quite genuinely not have known why she had been angry.

She hadn't been lying when she claimed that she was tired. Coming home and living with her parents was always exhausting. There were so many things she wanted to say to them that she couldn't.

She went upstairs slowly. Her bedroom had been redecorated along with the rest of the house and she had to admit that the coral and grey colour scheme was very attractive. The white furniture with its gilt trim had been a fourteenth birthday present. It was too fussy and frilly for her own taste, and even now she could remember how disappointed her mother had been at her lack of pleasure in the gift.

She looked at herself wryly in the full-length mirror. It was plainly obvious, surely, that she wasn't the frilly type. As a little girl, her mother had dressed her in frilly pastel dresses and matching pants, tying her strong, dark, remorselessly straight hair into soft bunches.

These days she dressed differently, in comfortable structured clothes that suited her tall narrow frame. She wore her dark hair in a curved bob, and no longer felt awkward or unfeminine because of her height.

At five nine she wasn't really that tall any more anyway, and she had learned at university that there were just as many men who liked tall slim girls as there were those who preferred small cuddly blondes.

The feeling of inferiority that not being the pretty little blonde daughter her mother had wanted had bred in her had disappeared completely while she was at university, and in its place she had developed a coolly amused distancing technique that held those men who wanted to get closer to her at an acceptable distance. She hadn't wanted any romantic involvements; marriage wasn't on her list of priorities. She had seen too much of what it could do to her sex in her own parents' marriage.

Even so, she hadn't been short of admirers; there were plenty of young men all too willing to date a girl who made it plain that marriage wasn't her sole purpose in life. Her mother often bemoaned the fact that she was, in her words, 'unfeminine', but there had been many men who had been drawn, rather than repulsed, by her cool indifference. So why, at twenty-five, was she still an inexperienced virgin?

It had been so long since she had given any thought at all to her virgin state that the fact that she should do so now shocked her. She walked from her bed to the window and stared blindly out of it. It had been the sound of the name Luke O'Rourke that had brought on this introspective mood, and she didn't need a psychiatrist to tell her why.

It had, after all, been Luke O'Rourke who had shattered her childish dreams and shown her the reality of sexual need and desire.

And it had also been Luke O'Rourke who had shown her what she wanted to do with her life, she reminded herself. How ironic it was, then, that she should hear his name mentioned now, when she was once again in a way at a crossroads in her life.

She was going to lose her job. Oh, it wasn't official yet,

but she knew it anyway. The conversation she had had with the head just before the school closed down for the long summer recess had been plain enough. They needed to shed staff; the part-timers wouldn't be coming back after the holiday, but that wasn't enough. Government cuts meant that the school still needed to lose one full-time teacher, and, as the head had uncomfortably but quite rightly pointed out, she was in the fortunate position of having parents who were financially both able and willing to support her.

Looking at the position from the head's point of view, she couldn't blame him. He was quite right in what he said, after all; if she stayed on at the school now, she would have to do so knowing that she was keeping a job from someone who badly needed the income that teaching brought. She moved restlessly round her room picking things up and then putting them down again. She hated the thought of giving up her job, but what alternative did she really have? It would be morally wrong of her to stay, knowing that in doing so she was depriving someone else of their living.

It was a similar dilemma to the one she had experienced in a much milder form when she first started teaching, and she had long ago decided that, when it came to her own background, her father's wealth and her mother's snobbery, she must just accept that these were things she could not change and must go on to live her own life, by her own rules.

She knew why Angus MacPherson had sent for her and talked to her as he had. He was counting on her doing the right thing, on her handing in her notice, and discreetly solving his over-staffing and financial problems for him, and she knew as well that she would. But knowing that she would be doing the right thing didn't ease the pain of knowing how much she would lose. She would have a period of notice to work—that was written into her contract—but it wouldn't be more than a month. The man who would take over her classes, would he sense the same burning desire to learn that she had seen beneath Johnny Bate's truculence? Would he see behind the wide blue eyes of Laura Holmes, with her already almost too-developed body, to the sharply incisive mind that Gemma had seen? There was no reason why he shouldn't, but so many of her colleagues had been ground down by their own problems and by the depressing poverty of the area they lived and worked in that they often no longer saw their pupils as individuals.

Unlike the majority of them, Gemma was single. She had the time to devote to her class outside the schoolroom. It wasn't just a job to her, and yet to use the word 'vocation,' even if only to herself, made her feel acutely uncomfortable.

Even so, she knew that it gave her a tremendous thrill to be able to impart knowledge to another mind, to witness its awakening and growth, and she had Luke O'Rourke to thank for that.

Luke O'Rourke. Of course it couldn't be the same man. The coincidence of the Luke O'Rourke she had known and her father's new business acquiantance both being in the construction industry was no more than just that. The Luke she had known had been nothing more than a labourer working as part of a gang of itinerants. She moved slowly round her bedroom, drifting back to her bed and sitting down on it, letting her mind take her back. Her fingers absently touched the bedspread that was now shiny and tailored in deep coral, but had once been soft baby pink, frilled and flounced.

It had been a hot dry summer that year, and she had been bored and restless, impatient of and embarrassed by her mother's petty snobbishness, and resentful of her father's masculine condescension. She had come home from school with high marks in all her classes, only to be told rather reprovingly by her father that girls didn't need to be clever and that they should certainly never be competitive, this last rebuke having been earned because she had done much better at school than her brother.

At fourteen she had sensed that she wasn't the daughter her parents wanted, although then she hadn't really known why. All she had known was that she felt constrained and uncomfortable in the persona they were tailoring for her. Her mother made her feel embarrassed when she went out shopping with her. Gemma didn't like the way she talked to the people in the shops who served her. Manchester was their nearest city, but her mother didn't shop there. She preferred Chester, but when Gemma asked her why, when it was so much smaller, all she would say was that it was much more 'our sort of place'. Occasionally her mother shopped in London and came back with dark green bags from Harrods. Gemma already knew that she had a privileged life; her father was fond of pointing out to her that not many daddies could afford to spoil their daughters the way he spoiled her, but Gemma was always left with the feeling that his gifts weren't given freely and that they had to be paid for. She also knew that somehow she disappointed him.

With the onset of puberty she was growing tall. Gangly was how her mother had described her. Her skin was smooth and faintly olive, her eyes a deeply serious grey. She often looked in the mirror and was puzzled that she didn't look more like her pretty blue-eyed and blonde-haired mother.

Her father was very dark and she knew that people thought her parents made a very attractive couple. Mrs Moreton, their daily, was always saying so.

David, two years older than her, had been sent away for the summer on a special adventure training course in the Welsh mountains. She would dearly have loved to go with him, but her father had frowned and told her that it wasn't suitable for girls.

'Oh, no, darling, it isn't at all ladylike,' her mother had told her when she pleaded to be allowed to go. There were very few children locally for her to play with and so she had been reduced to spending long hours alone riding her pony, Bess.

It was while on one of these sojourns that she had first met Luke ...

The Cheshire countryside, surrounding the village was pretty and criss-crossed with public footpaths and walks. In July the fields were heavy with their crops, a blue haze clouding the far distant Welsh hills to the west, and the Derbyshire peaks to the south east.

It was a hot afternoon, and Gemma was content to let fat little Bess amble along at her own pace. While she quite enjoyed riding, she was not strongly obsessed by it.

It had been her mother's idea that she learn to ride. Mrs Parish had seen it as the right sort of hobby for her daughter, expecting that it would lead to Gemma's inclusion amongst the rather stand-offish local county set, whose sons and daughters all learned to ride almost before they could walk, but these children were all taught at home, not at the exclusive riding establishment to which Gemma's parents sent her, and once she realised that the only people they were likely to meet through Gemma's riding were in much the same position as themselves she had soon lost interest in the whole idea.

Bess had been a tenth birthday present, and although her mother often now complained that the pony was an unnecessary expense, Gemma had insisted on keeping her. She was sturdily enough built to support Gemma's slim frame, even if her ever-growing legs did dangle rather dangerously either side of Bess's plump little body. The pony spent most of the year greedily enjoying the luxury of her comfortable paddock adjoining the house, good-naturedly ambling along the country lanes with Gemma on her back when she was at home at a pace not much faster than her rider could have walked.

Her destination on this occasion was a small wood where, the previous summer, she had seen a family of otters at play on the banks of the river that flowed through it. She found the clearing by the river easily enough, dismounting to tie Bess's reins to a handy tree trunk. Here the ground smelled hot and moist, the sun shading eerily through the umbrella of leaves overhead. Pine needles and other vegetation covered the ground, giving it a stringy texture. Although she couldn't see it, Gemma could hear the sound of the river. She felt in her pocket for the sandwiches she had brought with her, and the book. She could have read quite easily in the garden at home, but somehow she felt over-exposed and uncomfortable there, and if her mother came back early and caught her slopping around in her old shorts and T-shirt, she would complain.

Neither of her parents approved of Gemma wearing shorts or jeans; they both liked her to wear dresses, preferably with fluffily gathered skirts. Gemma hated them. She felt they looked ridiculous on her. All those frills with her arms and legs sticking out like thin sticks.

Although she was fourteen she had practically no figure at all yet. Not like some of the girls in her class. Well, she did have *some* figure. Her breasts had started to develop and she was wearing a bra, but she knew that her mother had been shocked to see how tall she had grown this last term.

She found a comfortable place to sit down not far from the river, her back supported by the trunk of an ancient oak. She felt in her pocket for her sandwiches, before spreading her jacket on the ground. They were doing Lawrence at school next term, and she had bought some paperbacks with her pocket money. English Lit. was one of her favourite subjects.

Within minutes she was so deeply engrossed that she was only aware of the intruder when she felt the cold drops of moisture from his skin fall on to her arm.

She looked up, her eyes widening in shock and alarm as they encountered the tall, muscular frame of the man standing looking down at her. He must have been swimming in the river, she realised, because droplets of water were running down over his chest still, darkening the springy mat of hair that grew there. He was wearing jeans that were old and very faded, but his feet were bare. His arms and torso as well as his face were burned dark by constant exposure to the sun. Tiny lines radiated outwards from the corners of his dark blue eyes. His hair clung sleekly to his scalp and it was very dark.

Gemma moistened her lips nervously, suddenly feeling extremely alarmed.

'It's all right, I'm not going to hurt you.'

His voice rumbled from the depth of his chest, but it was gentle and reassuring, tinged with an accent she recognised as Irish.

The moment she heard it Gemma felt herself relax. She knew instinctively and beyond any shadow of a doubt that he wasn't lying to her, and that he meant her no harm.

He looked down at the book she was reading and smiled at her. 'Lawrence, eh? Now there's a fine writer. Not as robust as some maybe, but a fine writer nonetheless.'

'Do you ... do you like reading, then?'

There had been an odd pause then while he looked at her for a moment, and then he had said quietly, 'I like it fine when I have the time.'

And that was how it had all begun.

CHAPTER TWO

IN retrospect, that afternoon seemed to have a fey, almost magical, quality to it.

Gemma remembered that she had offered to share her sandwiches with him and that he had equally gravely accepted.

She had learned that he was working with a gang of labourers on the new motorway that was being built several miles away. He liked the countryside, he had told her, and he preferred to be alone on his time off. His family had come originally from Ireland, but he had been orphaned as a child and brought up in a home. His whole face had hardened when he told her that, and he had added that he didn't intent to stay a labourer all his life. He had seemed so much older and more mature than she was herself that she had been half shocked to learn that he was only twenty years old.

He questioned her about herself, and she had told him openly and gravely about her background and her family.

In turn he had told her about his plans to educate himself, to start his own business. Labouring paid well, he had told her, but there was no future in it. It was a young man's work, and it was gruellingly hard. He had told her that he had had to leave school at sixteen and about the night-school courses he was taking, now finished for the summer.

'It's to be hoped I don't forget everything I've learned

before they start up again in the autumn.'

'I could help you remember.'

The diffident words were out before she could silence them, and she had tensed stiffly, waiting for him to laugh at her, or maybe even be angry. She had forgotten for a moment that men didn't like girls who were too clever and her eyes blurred with adolescent tears while her olive skin flamed a miserable scarlet in her embarrassment and shame.

When he had said softly, 'Maybe you could at that . . . and perhaps teach me a lot of the things I ought to know as well,' she had looked at him nervously, not sure whether he was being serious or making fun of her.

'I aim to make a success of my life,' he had told her fiercely, 'and if I'm to be that, I'll need to know things you can't learn from a book.'

'You mean things like using the right knife and fork?' Gemma had asked him intuitively.

'Yes, but not just that. You say your father's a master builder. There are things I need to know, books I need to read, if I'm ever going to be anything more than a labourer, and the building industry is the only one I know. The problem with this sort of life is that I never stay in one place long enough to do more than one full term at night school. If I had the right books, if I knew the right way to go about it, there's a lot that I could teach myself.'

Gemma had understood what he was trying to say and it would be easy enough for her to help him. Her father's study was full of just the sort of books he needed. David was to take her father's place in the company eventually, and every holiday her father drew up a syllabus of things he had to study.

Right from the start it was almost as though she had already known Luke all her life. She could talk to him about things she had never been able to discuss with anyone else, and within a week it seemed to Gemma that they had known one another all their lives.

It wasn't difficult for her to supply him with the books he needed, nor was it hard for her to slip away from the house most evenings to meet him. Even the weather was in their favour, remaining fine and warm so that they could meet in the clearing by the river.

She knew now that Luke lived in a caravan close by the motorway development and that he shared his accommodation with four other men. He liked to come to the river to swim because he claimed it was the only way he could feel really clean. The caravan boasted only one shower, which wasn't enough to wash away the ingrained dust and dirt of the backbreaking work of road building.

Of course she never mentioned him at home. She knew how deeply her parents would disapprove of their association. She wasn't even allowed to mingle with the village children, and Luke, with his Irish background, his accent and his lack of education could never be anyone her parents would approve of her knowing. Anyway, she preferred to keep their friendship a secret. It made it seem more special, more hers and hers alone, and she liked that. She felt comfortable with Luke, and she liked the glow of pleasure it gave her when she was able to give him some nugget of information he hadn't known. She had 'borrowed' an old picnic basket from the pantry, and with it she taught Luke the correct placings of knives, forks and spoons.

Together they explored the mystery of Hardy and the

pain of Lawrence, and together they laughed at Luke's mimicking of her accent and hers of his.

Because of him Gemma felt more at home with herself than at any other time in her life. Her legs and arms were now tanned a soft gold and when she was with Luke she forgot how tall and gangly she was. Luke didn't mind that she wasn't blonde and pretty. Sexual awareness as yet had no part in her life. She knew all about it, of course, but physical desire and all its mysteries were something she had yet to experience.

All that changed the day David came home and brought a friend with him. Tom Hardman was the most beautiful-looking human being Gemma had ever seen. He was the same age as David, just seventeen, but he was taller than her brother and broader, his skin sheened golden by their Welsh holiday, his hair thick and brightly fair, his eyes as blue as the August skies.

Gemma fell head over heels in love with him the moment she set eyes on him.

She didn't tell Luke about him. Not at first; the strange tummy-twisting sensation she had experienced the moment she set eyes on Tom was something still too private and wonderful to talk about to anyone, even Luke. She had barely been able to eat her supper last night, or her breakfast this morning. David had had his birthday while he was away, and as a present he had had driving lessons and a brand new car, and right after breakfast the two boys had set out in it.

Although she had ached to be asked to go with them, Gemma had not really expected it. David was fond enough of her in his way, but the three-year gap between them, and the insistence their parents put on the differing roles in life of their two opposite sexes, had made it impossible for them to be really close.

For the first time since she had met Luke, time seemed to hang heavily on Gemma's hands. She couldn't wait for evening to come and for the two boys to come back.

For the first time since they had met, she didn't go to meet Luke that evening. Instead, she stayed close to the house, waiting for David and Tom to come back. Only they didn't. At least not until late. Gemma's room overlooked the front of the house, and she heard them getting out of the car long after she had gone to bed. She slipped out from beneath her duvet and crept to the window to look down at them. Tom's blond hair shone in the clear moonlight. He was smiling at David, and Gemma wondered in tremulous awe what it would be like to be kissed by him.

She had heard the other girls at school talking about kissing, and other things, and she was suddenly impatient and despairing of her own inexperience. She was sure that Tom must have kissed lots of girls; even if he did kiss her she wouldn't know what to do ... not properly. She tried to imagine it, conjuring up images of what physical desire could be from all that she had read, but all she could think of was the paralysing embarrassment that would be hers if her nose got in the way, or worse still if Tom should guess that she didn't know how to kiss properly.

In the morning she overslept and got up just in time to see the two boys driving off.

Her mother smiled at her over the breakfast table, and said breathlessly, 'Tom is such a nice boy, and so good-looking. His family come from Scotland, and he's invited David up there to spend the last two weeks of the holiday with him.' A petulant frown suddenly creased her forehead as she looked at Gemma.

'Oh, Gemma, why are you wearing those awful jeans and not one of your pretty dresses? What on earth must Tom think of you? You'll have embarrassed poor David, as well. Why on earth can't you be like other girls? You're such a dreadful tomboy . . . not like my daughter at all, really.'

That afternoon, in the shade of the clearing, Gemma had been so preoccupied that at last Luke had put his book down and asked gently, 'What is it, Gemma? Is something wrong at home?'

She shook her head, suddenly feeling nervous and tongue-tied, glad when Luke didn't question her more closely.

They had continued to meet for the rest of Tom's stay, but something was different; Luke was different . . . more distant somehow but even though she noted this, it didn't really touch her. She was living, breathing, thinking Tom, and at last, on the very last day of his visit, he said carelessly at breakfast, 'Since it's my last night here tonight, David, why don't the three of us go out somewhere together?'

At first she was too paralysed to say a word. It was like a dream coming true. Tom was taking her out. Rosily her mind blotted out the fact that David would be with them, too, and that until now her hero had barely addressed more than a single word to her.

It was arranged that the three of them would go to a local barn dance that was held every week, and for the rest of the morning Gemma walked round in a state of ecstatic bliss.

It was only over lunch, which she and her mother ate

alone, that reality intruded.

'I don't know what on earth you're going to wear tonight,' her mother fussed. 'You haven't got anything to go out dancing in, really, apart from the dress you had for Christmas.'

The dress in question was fussy and little girlish and Gemma hated it, but her mother was right, there was nothing else she could wear. She had spent the summer in jeans and shorts, refusing to go shopping with her mother when asked, and now she had no alternative but to wear the hated pink frills.

And as the afternoon wore on, that wasn't the only thing to torment her. Suppose when they were out that Tom *did* want to kiss her? She had learned from the girls at school that a goodnight kiss at the end of a date was very much the expected thing. From glowing anticipation she went to abject dread. As much as she longed to feel Tom's mouth on hers, she also feared it. How awful it would be if he turned away from her in disgust, or worse still laughed at her. What on earth was she going to do?

The afternoon stretched endlessly in front of her, and she was glad to be meeting Luke; talking to him would give her something to occupy her mind.

He had been swimming, she saw when she reached the clearing. His jeans were splodged a darker blue where his skin had dampened them. They clung to his body in a way that made her aware of how much taller and stronger than either David or Tom he was.

The companionable silence they normally shared was missing today; she felt tense and on edge, barely aware of what he was saying to her, until, at last, he placed his hands on her shoulders and turned her to face him.

'Something's wrong with you, Gemma. Why don't you tell me what it is?'

She looked up at him uncertainly, blushing and then hanging her head.

'Is it me? Have I said something to upset you? Have I?'

She shook her head. 'No . . . no, it's nothing like that.' She looked at him and suddenly a solution to all her problems came to her. Relief spread through her, melting away her fear and tension.

She reached towards him instinctively, her hand on the warm, bare flesh of his arm.

'Oh, Luke, you've got to help me . . . please . . .'

'If I can.'

She saw him frown and was aware of the faint hesitation in his voice, and her courage almost deserted her. She took a deep breath and faced him bravely. 'Luke . . . would you . . . could you teach me how to kiss?'

She could almost feel the shock that ran through him and closed her eyes against the shamed surge of humiliation that coloured her skin. In Luke's company she had managed to forget that she was too tall and unfeminine, but now in his strained silence she saw all too plainly how little Luke or anyone else would want to kiss a girl like her. Of course Tom wasn't attracted to her. How could he be? Hadn't her mother told her often enough how plain she was?

Tears spurted into her eyes before she could stop them. She felt them squeezing through her tightly closed eyelids and splashing down on to her hot cheeks, but as she raised a clenched hand to rub them away, Luke caught hold of her.

'Stop crying, little one. I didn't mean to hurt you.' His

voice was rough and yet soft at the same time, and her tears turned to a strangled hiccup of laughter in her throat at the thought of anyone describing her as 'little', although compared with Luke's tall, heavy frame she supposed she was.

'Why this sudden desire to know how to kiss?' he asked her gently, but underneath his gentleness Gemma was aware of a certain tension within him, a slight withdrawal from her that she could sense but not explain.

One of his hands cupped the side of her face, his thumb wiping the tear stains from her skin.

'There'll be plenty of time for you to learn things like that.'

'No, there won't. Tom's leaving tomorrow morning.'

The mournful words made Luke frown at her, the comforting movement of his thumb ceasing. It struck her suddenly that there was something extraordinarily pleasant about having him touch her. Her father was not a physically affectionate man, and she had never particularly wanted his touch, but now she had an inexplicable desire to move closer to Luke and to be held within the comfort of his arms.

'Tom? Who's Tom?' he asked her sharply, dispelling her mood.

'He's a friend of my brother's. He's staying with us. The three of us are going out tonight, to a barn dance at Winston.'

She looked up just in time to catch the smile that curled Luke's mouth. There was an expression on his face that she didn't recognise. It made her shiver as though she had suddenly gone cold.

'And it's this Tom you really want to kiss you, is that

it?' His mouth twisted, the dark blue eyes no longer smiling at her, but frighteningly hard. 'Then he's the one you should be asking for lessons, not me.'

He made to get up, and Gemma knew instinctively that he was going to leave. She had made him angry, and that was the last thing she wanted to do. She could feel fresh tears clogging her throat, and she reached up blindly, tugging on his arm.

'No. Please, Luke, you don't understand. If Tom kisses me, he'll know that I've never done it before. He'll laugh at me ...' She shivered as he stopped trying to move away and instead looked down into her eyes.

'I know that I'm not ... not pretty, or anything ... and you don't have to kiss me if you really don't want to ... but ... but ...' She was struggling against a fresh wave of misery, stumbling over the words as she fought against her fear that she had somehow angered him and might lose his friendship, and her need to explain to him just how much she needed his help.

Without being able to explain why, she knew instinctively that when it came to kissing Luke would know exactly what to do. What he did when he left her in the evenings, and where he went when he wasn't working, was something they never discussed, but with an age-old female intuition that her body recognised, even if her mind could not yet do so, deep down inside Gemma knew that Luke was a man who would appeal to her sex.

'No, you're not pretty.' He said it roughly, as though something had got stuck in his throat, and when she looked up at him in hurt misery, he veiled his eyes with his lashes. They were dark and very thick, casting shadows on the deep bronze of his skin. He smelled of fresh air and growing things, of sunshine, and something else she couldn't define but that she liked, Gemma recognised as he moved slightly towards her.

His hands curved round her upper arms, his fingers pressing against their bare flesh. He had touched her like this several times before, but now she knew immediately that this was different.

'All right, little girl, if this is really what you want.' They were both sitting down, but now Luke was leaning towards her, blotting out the sunlight. He wasn't wearing a shirt because he had been swimming, and he was so close to her that she could feel the heat of the sun coming off his skin.

His hands moved up her arms, his thumbs probing the firmness of her shoulders beneath the thin covering of her T-shirt.

For some reason her heart had started to pound heavily, and she couldn't drag her gaze away from his face. He looked different somehow, not the Luke she knew. He was looking at her mouth, she realised, with a sudden jerking leap of her heart. She opened it to say his name and then closed it again, reminding herself stoically that this was what she had wanted.

Her heart was pumping frantically against the wall of her chest; with every breath she took, she half expected it to leap into her throat and choke her. If she felt like this in Luke's arms, how on earth was she going to feel when she was with Tom? She closed her eyes and shivered.

'Open your eyes, Gemma. It's not *him* who's teaching you to kiss, it's me.'

The harshness of Luke's voice made her obey his command immediately, her own eyes registering the shock of seeing the brittle fury in his.

'That's your first lesson,' he told her softly. 'No man likes the woman in this arms to pretend that she's with someone else.'

'I thought I was supposed to close my eyes,' Gemma protested chokily. 'They always do in films.'

'Maybe, but I like to see the effect I'm having on a girl when I kiss her.'

Although it was still rough, something about Luke's voice seemed to have changed; now it was like the throaty purr of a lion, Gemma thought dreamily: hypnotic and ever so faintly dangerous.

His face came nearer, and her fingers clutched nervously at his arms. His hands moved, sliding beneath her, one cupping the back of her head, the other holding her waist. Her lips felt dry, and yet somehow swollen. She swallowed nervously and then exhaled in shaky relief as she felt his lips move gently against her forehead, his breath warm on her skin.

His mouth was as delicate and gentle as a summer breeze as it teased her skin. She could feel the hard pad of his thumb, stroking against her jaw, and caressing the soft skin of her throat. He moved away from her a little, studying her flushed face, his mouth . . .

She shivered suddenly as she stared at his mouth, her hand lifting so that her fingers could touch it, her eyes looking wonderingly into his. When he drew the soft tips of her fingers into his mouth and gently sucked them, her wonder changed to stomach-jerking shock. The oddest of sensations burst into life inside her. Her breasts . . . She tore her eyes from his, dragging air into her compressed lungs as she looked down at her own body.

As though Luke knew everything she was feeling, he drew her into his arms, soothing her.

'It's all right ... don't worry ...'

How had he known what had happened to her? She could feel herself shaking as he rocked her gently. Her whole body felt flushed and strange, her wide-eyed, half-frightened gaze meshing with his as he held her away from him.

'Would you like me to stop?'

Would she? Could she endure to go all through this again with someone strange, someone who wouldn't understand like Luke did? She shook her head in dogged determination, her voice husky and strained as she whispered, 'No ... No ... I want you to go on.'

Trust replaced the fright in her eyes as she looked up at him. 'I know you don't really want to kiss me, Luke, but if you won't teach me, how can I ever learn?'

'The usual way,' he told her drily, 'by trial and error.'

'But boys don't like me.'

She felt the all-too-easy tears rise inside her again, and buried her head against Luke's hard shoulder. His skin smelled faintly male and alien, and yet conversely the contact was also reassuring. She felt Luke move her and opened her eyes to find that his mouth was only a whisper away from her own. She could feel her lips trembling and she pressed them together firmly, trying to get the trembling to stop.

Suddenly panic seized her and she wanted to tell him that she had changed her mind, but it was already too late, his mouth was touching hers, his lips caressing the closed, tight line of hers. His mouth felt warm and soft, but firm, too, and she quivered beneath the sensations clamouring inside her. He was stroking her mouth with tiny, teasing kisses that made her lips swell and soften. When she felt his tongue run along their tightly closed outline she quivered visibly, curling her nails into his flesh.

'Open your mouth, Gemma.'

His eyes stared into hers, mesmerising her, making her lips open so that he could . . .

Every reasoning faculty she possessed was suspended beneath the sensations rocking her. She had seen people kissing like this in films and on television, and privately she had always thought it faintly yucky, but now that she was experiencing it for herself . . . She clung to him eagerly, letting his mouth tutor hers, quivering in eager excitement when his tongue stroked hers. That same peculiar ache she had felt in her breasts before was back, and it seemed as though Luke knew about it, too, because he stopped kissing her, briefly, to take her more fully into his arms, so that her breasts were pressing against his chest. When he kissed her his whole body moved and it made her want to rub herself against him.

She had forgotten why she had asked him to kiss her; she had forgotten everything but the sweet surge of passion flooding through her body, her eyes dark and heavy with the force of it, her lips moist and swollen. She wanted him to kiss her again, and again, but suddenly his body was tensing and he was drawing away from her, his chest expanding and contracting rapidly as he drew in air.

'Luke.' She reached out to touch him but he moved away from her.

'I think you've learned enough for one lesson.' He was looking at her as though he was angry with her. 'Although I warn you, if you react like that to every boy who kisses you, soneone's going to have to pin a notice on you warning them that you're under sixteen.'

It took a few seconds for his meaning to get through to her, but, when it did, she flushed blood-red, and stumbled clumsily to her feet. Suddenly everything seemed all wrong; the magic of those moments in his arms was spoiled and sullied, and she wanted to run from him and hide herself away. He was telling her that she had behaved wantonly. The reason for the tension she had felt in her body and her innocent desire to get as close to him as she possibly could suddenly became unpleasantly clear to her.

He saw the expressions chase one another across her face, and frowned. 'Gemma ...'

It was too late for him to apologise now. He had ruined everything between them; he had made her feel ... dirty, she thought, choking, moving slowly back from him as he got up and came towards her, holding out his hand.

'Gemma, listen to me.'

'No.' Her voice sounded strained and shocked. 'I think I hate you, Luke,' she said bitterly. 'And I don't want to see you ever again.' She turned round and ran from him to where she had left Bess tethered before he could stop her, loud sobs tearing at her throat. She knew that he had followed her, and when she scrambled up on to Bess's plump back he reached for her.

'No ... No, don't touch me.' She hit out at him wildly, tears streaming down her face. He had spoilt something that had been unbearably precious to her, something that her developing instincts told her was rare and special, and she couldn't wait to get away from him.

Wisely he let her go, sensing that to try and talk to her

in her present state of near hysteria would do no good at all.

By the time she was close to home, she had herself under proper control. She stopped once to scrub at her damp face with a grubby handkerchief, and luckily when she got back her mother was still out.

All the anticipation and excitement with which she had viewed the evening was gone. She prepared for it with a feeling of resignation rather than pleasure, and, irrationally, it was Luke she blamed for her change of heart. Luke had spoiled it all for her by being so nasty to her.

She couldn't let herself think about those moments in his arms. Half of her wanted to pretend that they hadn't really happened, because she knew, even if she didn't want to admit it, that now that they had, they had changed everything between them, and she didn't want things to change, she wanted them to go on being friends. But how could they be friends when she knew that secretly Luke despised her? He must despise her, mustn't he? Girls didn't go around asking people to kiss them, did they?

All through the rest of the afternoon she goaded herself with recriminations and contempt.

After dinner she and the boys went up to their rooms to change. Defiantly she decided that she might as well wear her jeans. It was, after all, a barn dance, and so what if everyone mistook her for a boy? She didn't care.

She wasn't allowed as yet to wear make-up, and she looked miserably at her reflection in the mirror once she was ready.

Her jeans were old and worn, the denim soft and faded. Used to her mother's condemnation of her tall, slim body, she didn't see the way the denim followed the long lines of her legs, and the smallness of her waist.

David banged on her door as he and Tom went downstairs, and knowing that she couldn't delay any longer she hurriedly brushed her hair and went after them.

'Gemma, you can't go out looking like that! I thought you were going to wear a dress.'

Both her parents were looking disapprovingly at her, and Gemma hovered on the verge of saying that she had decided she didn't want to go after all, but to her surprise David came to her rescue, saying lightly, 'It's a barn dance, Mum. All the others will be dressed casually. She looks fine.'

Both boys were also wearing jeans, and although Gemma could see that her mother wasn't pleased, she made no further comment.

Since Tom had already passed his driving test, it had been decided that on this occasion he would drive. Gemma sat in the back of her brother's small car, wondering why she did not feel more excited as they drove towards their destination.

The dance was being held in the village hall. Several cars were already parked outside it, and they could hear the noise from the group as they got out of the car.

Inside the hall was hot and busy with gyrating bodies. The atmosphere was very smoky, and stung Gemma's eyes. David found them a table while Tom went to the bar and got them all a drink. Gemma had asked for an orange juice and she noticed when he came back with their drinks that Tom wasn't having anything alcoholic either.

When David laughed at him, Tom reminded him that he was driving.

Gemma couldn't help noticing that more than one girl looked across to their table, and she tried to contain her feeling of desertion when David tapped Tom on the arm and drew his attention to a couple of girls standing watching the dancers.

'You'll be OK here on your own for a while, won't you?' David asked her as they got up. And, as he and Tom moved away, to her chagrin Gemma heard her brother saying to his friend, 'I'm sorry that Ma was so insistent that we bring her with us.'

So Tom hadn't wanted her company at all, she thought miserably. It had all been arranged by her mother.

She watched as the hall filled up and her brother and Tom kept on dancing with the same two girls. She was so engrossed in her own feeling of misery and self-loathing that she didn't even look up when the shadow fell across her line of vision.

It took the sound of her name to drag her attention away from the dancers and to the person standing in front of her.

'Luke!' The unexpectedness of him being there, coupled with the fact that he had no doubt witnessed the humiliating fact that she was on her own, put the final seal of misery on the evening.

'Enjoying yourself?'

He had to know that she wasn't, she thought bitterly, tossing her head in defiant misery as she replied in a brittle voice, 'Yes, thanks, are you?'

She saw him shrug, the gesture implying a certain amount of amused disdain as he looked around.

'It's not really my sort of thing.'

'No, I don't suppose it is.'

All the frustration and misery of the day poured out in her voice, two spots of colour staining her skin, her eyes glittering with temper and pain as she said disdainfully, 'I'm surprised they allowed you in here. Most places seem to have banned the navvies from the motorway.'

She was repeating something she had heard her father say about the men from the road gangs, and the moment the cruel words had left her mouth she was horrified and disgusted with herself. Dimly she recognised that all her pain and misery was somehow connected with Luke and that it was because of this that she had hit out at him, but as she watched the quiet contempt settle in his eyes and saw him step away from her, she knew with bitter self-knowledge that she had driven him away, and that she had spoilt their friendship.

As he walked away from her she stood up and called his name, but either he didn't hear her, or he didn't care, because he didn't stop.

After he had gone her eyes felt heavy with tears. Losing Luke's friendship mattered far more to her than the fact that her mother had arranged for her to be here with Tom. In fact Tom, and her feelings for him, suddenly seemed to be the least important thing in her life. How could she have spoken like that to Luke? No wonder he had looked at her the way he did. Tomorrow afternoon she would apologise and explain to him. Just thinking that tomorrow she would see him made her feel better.

When the two boys eventually came back to the table, she was astounded to hear Tom ask her to dance.

They had dancing lessons at school, and it was

something she was surprisingly good at.

They left at twelve o'clock, Tom and Gemma going out to the car first, leaving David to follow. When they reached the shadows thrown by the buildings, Gemma was astounded when Tom suddenly and clumsily took her in his arms, pressing his mouth wetly against hers.

His kiss wasn't anything like Luke's. In fact she found that she hated it; hated the wetness of his mouth, and the jarring sensation of his teeth bumping against her own. As quickly as she could she freed herself from his embrace, trembling with a mixture of disgust and anger. She could see that Tom was chagrined by her lack of response, but she no longer cared. Why on earth had she ever thought he was handsome? He wasn't at all. Not when she compared him to Luke . . . Luke. She stopped dead yards away from the car, feeling her tummy begin to flutter and her heart start to leap violently in her chest. If she closed her eyes she could wipe away the memory of Tom's kiss by conjuring up the things she had felt when Luke kissed her. She shivered slightly, aching for him to be there with her.

Her last thought as she closed her eyes that night was that soon it would be morning. Soon she could be with Luke.

CHAPTER THREE

ONLY it hadn't been like that, Gemma reflected grimly, coming out of her reverie and walking over to her bedroom window. When she had gone to the clearing that afternoon Luke hadn't been there, nor the afternoon after, nor the one after that. And so it had gone on for more than a week before she finally accepted that Luke wasn't going to come back, and that through her own folly she had destroyed something infinitely precious.

She must have hurt him very badly indeed, she now recognised with the wisdom of maturity. She had after all thrown in his face the very thing he was fighting so hard to overcome, and his reaction to her cruel taunt had been very much the same as hers would have been had he, for instance, mocked her for her most private insecurities.

She had deserved to lose his friendship. She sighed faintly and stared out unseeingly at the landscape.

Could the Luke she had known and this man her mother had mentioned be one and the same person? Perhaps it was not so far fetched that they might after all. Luke had often expressed to her his desire and determination to make a success of his life. He had had the intelligence to do it, and the willpower. If he was the same person ... She felt her heart leap like a salmon leaping upriver, and a wry smile twisted her mouth.

If he was, she doubted that he would be all that pleased to see her—if he remembered her. The summer had been spoilt for her when he had gone, but she had recognised that she had deserved to lose his friendship, and she hadn't made any attempt to seek him out, fearing a further rebuff.

Now when she thought about him it was with a mingling of gratitude and embarrassment. He had been very kind to her. She squirmed a little with embarrassment at the memory of how she had asked him to teach her how to kiss, aware of her very contradictory emotions at the thought of seeing him again.

One part of her hoped that he had made a success of his life and achieved everything that he had wanted, while the other ... Even now, she still blushed for her fourteen-year-old self.

She heard a car coming up the drive, and realised that her mother was on her way back.

David and Sophy arrived soon afterwards, Sophy exclaiming enviously over Gemma's outfit.

'You're so lucky to be so tall and slim.' She made a wry face. 'I never manage to look elegant.'

Gemma could see the surprise in her mother's eyes. She wasn't used to other women envying her daughter. In her view, of the two, Sophy was by far the more attractive. Couldn't she see that small Sophy might well have a weight problem later in life? Gemma wondered wryly, standing up and excusing herself.

'Don't forget, will you, darling, that Daddy's bringing people home for dinner,' her mother called after her as she headed for the hall.

Behind her Gemma heard David asking, 'Anyone I

know?' while Sophy chirruped that she had better go home and get changed.

She could see why her parents were so pleased about David's marriage, Gemma reflected as she walked into her bedroom. Sophy would make him exactly the right sort of wife. David wasn't like her. He had never questioned their parents' values, or their way of life. David wanted a wife like their mother and in Sophy, Gemma suspected that he had probably found her. Although Sophy was, as her mother termed it, 'well connected', her aunt was relatively poor. Gemma hadn't missed the faintly avaricious gleam in Sophy's eyes when she talked about their new home and the Spanish apartment that her parents had given them as part of their wedding present.

What was the matter with her? she asked herself as she showered. People married for all sorts of different reasons and it wasn't up to her to question or criticise David's and Sophy's motives.

She dressed for dinner with unusual care. It had been a long time since she had been the awkward teenager who had stubbornly refused to wear anything but jeans. It was true that her dinner dates were few and far between, but she had discovered in the years since she had left home that she had quite a flair for choosing the right sort of clothes for her slender height.

The outfit that Sophy had admired, for instance, had been bought as separates from two different shops. The sleek, fitted, fine wool black skirt was one that she could either dress up or down. With it she had been wearing a soft off-white silk-satin blouse, and over that an unstructured black and white open-checked wool jacket.

It had rather surprised her to discover that she liked clothes. As a teenager she had tended to despise her mother's concentration on them but once she had broken free of her own belief that, because she wasn't the daughter her parents wanted her to be, she was ugly she had found that she enjoyed hunting round the shops looking for bargains that helped to stretch out her slender means.

The fact that she was a perfect size ten helped, because it meant that she was often able to buy end-of-the-season models at a very good price.

For dinner she decided to wear a pretty silk suit with a fluid pleated skirt that buttoned provocatively down one side. Its jacket had long cuffed sleeves and a demure Peter Pan collar.

The soft peach colour suited her tawny skin and hair. A mischievous grin tilted the corners of her mouth as she swept the silken length of her hair up into a sophisticatedly casual knot that left soft tendrils framing her face and showed off the delicacy of her tiny ears.

Her only jewellery was the pearl necklet her parents had bought her for her twenty-first birthday, with its matching earrings, and the very plain gold watch they had given her when she left university. The plainness of both these gifts had been bewailed by her mother and father. Hugh Parish liked spoiling his women, but Gemma had been adamant. The only other present she had allowed her parents to buy for her was her small car.

Her father had a 'thing' about punctuality and Gemma knew better than to be late going down for dinner. As she had known she would, she found David and her parents in the drawing-room, her mother and brother talking about the wedding while her father dispensed drinks.

These business dinners had been a feature of their lives for as long as Gemma could remember. Her father preferred to bring his clients home to wine and dine them rather than to use anonymous restaurants. Although her mother was a first-class cordon bleu cook, when her parents entertained, her father always hired staff.

She could see both her parents registering surprise at the way she was dressed and she hid a small smile. Normally when she came home it was only on a very brief visit and she normally dressed for comfort rather than elegance.

'Why, darling, you look really lovely, doesn't she, Hugh?'

'She certainly does. What will you have to drink, Gemma?'

She didn't really like alcohol, and would have preferred a white wine spritzer, but knowing her father's views on all things 'modern' and as far as he was concerned 'faddish', she opted for a dry sherry.

Even that caused a rather raised eyebrow. In her father's opinion women preferred sweet sherry, but he poured a glass of pale amber liquid for her without any comment.

The doorbell rang, and David put down his gin. 'That will probably be Sophy. I'll go and let her in.'

Sophy had changed into a dress that Gemma easily recognised as being chosen by her mother. Sophy should really have been her mother's child and not her, she reflected, watching the two women as they discussed the floral arrangements for the wedding.

The doorbell rang again and this time her father went to answer it, ushering in two middle-aged couples, whom he introduced to Gemma as Moira and Harvey Goldberg, and Frances and James Hart.

'Harvey and James are business associates of your father's in this latest Portuguese development,' Susan Parish explained to Gemma as the four men started to discuss business and their wives gravitated towards Sophy to ask her how she was feeling about the forthcoming 'big day'.

'Senhor Armandez, their Portuguese associate, was over last week to report on progress to them,' Gemma heard her mother saying to her.

'Dad seems to have made quite a success of his overseas ventures.'

'Well, yes, but he hasn't made anything like as much as Luke O'Rourke is going to make from his development in the Caribbean. He's developing some land there that he bought, and your father's hoping that he might be able to persuade Luke to subcontract some of the development out to him.'

The doorbell rang again, surprising Gemma, who thought that everyone must have arrived. Her father had been frowning slightly as he listened to Harvey Goldberg discussing the progress being made on the Portuguese development, but now his frown relaxed, and a rather relieved smile lit his eyes as he excused himself and went to greet the late arrival.

Gemma knew who he was even before she saw him. The years might have obliterated the soft Irish accent she remembered, but the voice was still unmistakable, deep and measured.

From where she was standing she had a completely uninterrupted view of Luke as he walked into the room. Just for a moment she experienced the most peculiar sensation of *déjà vu*, while the room turned topsy-turvy on her, and then gradually as it straightened again she was forced to admit that although her Luke O'Rourke and her father's were one and the same man, he had changed considerably from the twenty-year-old she had known.

There was no mistaking the immaculate cut and fit of his Savile Row suit, or his handmade leather shoes. His shirt had probably come from Turnbull and Asser, and his tie wouldn't have looked out of place on the chairman of one of the major banks.

He looked nothing like the jean-clad man she remembered, and yet he was indubitably the same person.

The lines round his eyes had deepened slightly, and his hair was immaculately cut and groomed. His face and hands were tanned, but it wasn't the tan of a man who worked outside in all weathers now, but the tan of a man who spent long periods of time in much hotter climates.

Gemma watched as Luke smiled at her mother, and then more formally acknowledged her father's introductions to his business partners.

'David and Sophy of course you already know, but I don't think that you and Gemma, my daughter, have met.'

Gemma opened her mouth to tell her father that he was wrong and then closed it again obediently as she caught the warning glint in Luke's eyes.

It stunned her that he didn't want to recognise their old friendship, and although she wasn't aware of it her eyes clouded faintly with hurt, as she withdrew her hand from his strong grasp.

'No, unfortunately we have not.'

His voice was deep enough to send small shivers of sensation dancing along her nerves, which was surely rather odd, because she had never reacted to him like this before. She missed that soft touch of brogue in his voice, she realised as she listened to him; it had made him seem softer ... more approachable. And then her face burned hotly as she caught him looking at her. At her mouth, she realised, as she took a hurried step backwards. And she knew why. He was letting her know that he had not forgotten that last meeting between them.

God, the embarrassment of it! It had been bad enough to contemplate seeing him again when she had thought he was still the Luke she had known, but this man ... this Luke ... this sophisticated, successful and very male man was really a stranger to her. A stranger whom she had begged to teach her how to kiss, she thought feverishly.

'Gemma teaches.'

She dragged her attention away from Luke and looked at her father. He said it as though he felt he ought to apologise for her, but despite his *bonhomie* she sensed that he wasn't relaxed with Luke. Luke after all was not what her father would have termed 'our sort'.

'Oh,' Moira Goldberg smiled at her. 'Do you work locally then?'

Gemma could see that the American woman expected

to hear that she taught at some small and exclusive prep or nursery school. If she hadn't been so conscious of Luke watching her, she might almost have derived some amusement from the look in the older woman's eyes when she replied calmly, 'Not really. I work in Manchester, at a large comprehensive.'

But not for much longer, she acknowledged bitterly, unaware that her eyes had clouded again and that Luke was still watching her.

On the surface the meal was like many another business dinner she had suffered at her parents' insistence, but all the time she was so acutely conscious of Luke seated on her right. She had to fight the temptation to turn her head and stare at him, to register at close quarters the difference in him.

After an hour and a half of Luke talking to her with the courtesy and distance that more than upheld his claim to her father that they had never met, Gemma painfully accepted the fact that, as far as Luke was concerned, their old friendship might never have been.

She had been half expecting it, of course. Luke was obviously a very successful and wealthy man, and she supposed that it was only natural that he should want to leave the hardship of the past behind him, but it still hurt that he could treat her as though she were a complete stranger.

She had a sudden and very clear picture of Luke as he had been, of his humour and determination.

'You looked as though you had gone a long way from us, Gemma,' she heard him saying, and turned to look at him just in time to register the cool mockery of the look he was giving her. 'Pleasant thoughts I trust, whoever and whatever they were about.'

'Oh, Gemma always was a terrible daydreamer,' her mother interrupted with a warning look at her.

After Luke's remoteness at the dinner table, Gemma was surprised when, following dinner, he excused himself to her father and the other two men and came over to where she was standing in front of the open patio window.

'So you're a teacher, Gemma. Do you enjoy your job?'

Her chin tilted, her eyes wary as she met the mocking scrutiny in his.

'Yes, I do . . . very much.'

He smiled, and she was immediately conscious of how sensual his mouth was. The thought shocked her. She must have looked at it a hundred or more times before, but never with the awareness that jolted through her now. She could barely drag her gaze away. Impossible to think that that mouth had ever touched hers . . . had ever tutored and caressed . . .

'Gemma, darling, why don't you show Luke the rose garden? You can only really truly appreciate their scents at night,' her mother told Luke, as she urged the pair of them towards the patio, causing Gemma to grit her teeth against her obviousness. Surely her mother couldn't really be trying to pair her and Luke off with one another?

She was seething with a mixture of chagrin and resentment when Luke smiled warmly at her mother, for all the world as though there was nothing he wanted more than to fall in with her plans.

She was ready to burst out with an impassioned protest there and then, but the firm grip of his fingers on her arm stopped her, and it was only when they were out of earshot and sight of the drawing-room that he asked curtly,

'What's wrong, Gemma? Aren't I socially acceptable enough to be here with you, is that it?'

His accusation took the breath from her lungs, leaving her to stare at him in dumbfounded shock.

When she did get her breath back she stared furiously at him through the soft dusk. 'I don't think I'm following your line of reasoning, Luke. *You* were the one who didn't want to acknowledge me in there, remember. I'm not the one who doesn't want to remember that the two of us were once friends.'

'If I'd told your father that we already knew one another, he would have wanted to know how and where we met,' Luke countered coolly. 'Somehow I don't think he would have been too pleased to learn that his teenage daughter spent almost an entire summer alone in the company of a "road gang navvy", do you?'

His harsh repetition of the insult she had flung at him the last time they had met made her swallow hard. She had known at the time that her words had been unforgivable, but now, somehow, looking into his tightly bitter face, it was too late to tell him that she had never really meant them at all, and to ask for his forgiveness.

'I couldn't believe it when my mother mentioned your name. At first I thought you could never ...'

'Have made it to the top of the ladder?' he suggested smoothly. 'Why not? I told you I was going to. Didn't you believe me, Gemma?'

She frowned, troubled by something in his voice, but unable to name it.

'Yes ... Yes, of course I did ...'

She suddenly felt unutterably tired. She put out her hand in a weary gesture of defeat and unhappiness.

'Luke, we were once such good friends, and now ... I don't blame you if you hate me for what I said ... what I ... what I did.' She had to look away from him then. 'I ...' She felt herself flushing like a schoolgirl as he moved, and his hand cupped the side of her face, exerting a firm pressure that forced her to turn back into the light.

She had already noticed his clean, well-cared-for nails, but the palms of his hands weren't soft and flaccid; the skin was hard and faintly calloused and she found it comforting that there was still after all something of the old Luke left.

'You're still embarrassed about asking me to teach you how to kiss ... is that what you're trying to say?'

It was part of it, but not the most important part; but still it was a start, and she swallowed hard, and nodded her head.

To her chagrin he laughed, the sound warm, and vibrantly masculine. 'Ah, little innocent Gemma. If you must know, I was very tempted to teach you far more than just how to kiss.'

While she was still trying to assimilate that, he added carelessly, 'You'll never know just how much I needed the ego boost of having *you* ask *me* to teach you something. It always seemed as though the boot was on the other foot. I owe you a lot,' he told her quietly. 'Your faith in me ... your encouragement and help; they were what gave me the impetus to go on.'

'I was unforgivably rude to you,' Gemma told him in a quiet voice, biting her lip. 'I didn't really mean what I said to you, you know, Luke.'

'It doesn't really matter if you did.' The smile he gave her was carelessly amused. 'I'm not ashamed of my humble beginnings you know, Gemma. Now, we've talked enough about me and the past. Tell me about you. You teach at a Manchester comprehensive.' One eyebrow rose. 'By choice, or . . .'

'By choice,' Gemma told him firmly, her eyes suddenly darkening as she remembered that she would soon no longer have a job.

'What's wrong?' He had obviously picked up on her mood.

'Oh nothing really, it's just that I saw my headmaster before term finished, and he has to shed one full-time member of staff.'

Without meaning to do so, Gemma found that she was confiding to Luke the dilemma she was in, just as she had confided in him in the past.

'Have you told your parents?'

She made a negative gesture and shook her head. 'No, they wouldn't understand. They don't like me working there as it is.' She pulled a wry face. 'Mother would prefer me to teach somewhere more suitable, or, even better, to find myself a husband and settle down and produce children.'

'And you don't want that? You intend to remain single all your life?'

The question pulled her up short. It was true that she wasn't ready to marry yet, but it was also true that she had always hoped at some point that she would meet a man with whom she could share her life on equal terms; someone whom she could love and who would love her in return.

Suddenly she was all too aware of the paucity of her personal emotional life, and because she knew instinctively that Luke was a man who would never be short of the adulation of the opposite sex, she hid the truth from him and said lightly instead, 'Why not? It isn't against the rules these days.'

His eyebrows rose again.

'It is as far as your parents are concerned,' he pointed out, adding thoughtfully, 'So what will you do? I take it you *are* going to hand in your notice.'

'I don't feel I have much option.'

'Oh, there's always an option,' Luke told her drily. 'You could always refuse to be manoeuvred into leaving, and play a "wait and see" game.'

'Someone has to go, and if I don't leave, it could be someone else, someone who simply can't afford to lose their job,' Gemma pointed out desolately.

'You're too soft-hearted, Gemma,' Luke mocked her lightly. 'Maybe you should have settled for marriage to Tom Hardman, or someone like him, after all.'

'Tom Hardman?'

She saw the white gleam of his teeth in the fast encroaching darkness. 'Wasn't that his name?' he asked obliquely, and Gemma realised that he was talking about David's friend, and that long-ago summer.

'Yes,' she agreed, 'but ...'

'I think we'd better go in.' He took her arm in a firm, but detached grip, that nevertheless set off small tingles of reaction all through her body.

'We don't want to worry your mother, do we?' he taunted her as he escorted her towards the house. 'I don't think somehow that she quite approves of me.'

So he, too, had sensed that, despite her mother's surface gush and friendliness, underneath she felt differently. What could she say? Not the truth, which was that her mother was prepared to tolerate him because of his business influence. Luke was intelligent enough to know that for himself.

God, how stupid and unthinkingly cruel people like her parents could be! She frowned as Luke opened the patio door for her and stepped to one side to allow her to precede him inside.

He was right behind her, and as he started to step forward his hand touched her waist, lightly checking her.

'"Chapter Four. A gentleman on all occasions allows a lady to precede him, having first checked that the way is clear for her to do so."'

He bent his head so that she could feel the warmth of his breath against her ear, as well as hear the words. Only the firm pressure of his hand stopped her from whirling round in amazement. He was quoting word for word, as far as she could remember, from the book of etiquette she had brought him from the library, and his voice was full of hidden laughter as he did so.

She felt her own spirits rise and she managed to turn her head and look at him. He *was* laughing; she could see it in his eyes, and she felt light-hearted enough to tease him back in return.

'On this ocasion the gentleman did not look hard enough. My mother is heading this way.'

'Ah well, in that case, I'm afraid I'm going to be extremely ungentlemanly and leave her to you, while I join your father.'

Her mother looked flustered and also rather concerned, Gemma recognised, and she wondered again at the petty snobbishness that ruled her parents' lives.

'Gemma, darling, there you are! Where on earth have you been?'

Gemma would have thought the answer to that question was self-evident with Luke walking away from her, but even so she replied as calmly as she could. 'In the garden with Luke. You sent us there—remember?'

Instantly her mother's frown deepened. 'Gemma, I must warn you. Luke O'Rourke isn't the sort of man your father and I would have anything to do with if it wasn't for the fact that he and your father have business connections. He's not our sort at all, my dear, and he doesn't have a very good reputation where women are concerned. He isn't married of course, but ... we ... one hears quite a lot of gossip about him. He ...'

Gemma had had enough. She could feel her anger increasing with every word her mother uttered, and if she wasn't going to have an outright quarrel with her, now was the time for her to interrupt.

'Mother, I think I'm old enough and wise enough to know when a man's trying to inveigle me into his bed, and I can assure you that Luke wasn't, if that's what's worrying you.'

'Gemma, really!' Her mother looked round hastily, as though afraid that someone might have overheard.

'What am I supposed to do, ignore him?'

Her mother's mouth compressed. 'Gemma, you are

deliberately misunderstanding me. Luke O'Rourke is well known as a womaniser, and even if he wasn't, he's simply not our sort. No one knows who his family was.'

'Does it matter?' Gemma asked her hardily.

Her mother's mouth thinned again. 'Of course, one must admire the fact that he's built up his business practically from nothing, but that doesn't alter the fact that he isn't one of us.'

Gemma had to grit her teeth together to stop herself from screaming. This was the side of her mother she detested the most. Her parents' blinkered snobbishness caught at Gemma's throat and made her long to point out to her mother that the upper-middle classes didn't have an exclusive patent on brains and intelligence and that many of the people her mother so admired for coming from what she so archaically described as 'old money' were in fact the descendants of those Victorian entrepreneurs who had risen from obscurity to great wealth with the shipping, coal and railway industries.

'We have to have him round here occasionally, of course, and your father insisted on inviting him to the wedding.' Privately she was beginning to wonder if she had done the right thing in seating Gemma beside Luke O'Rourke for the wedding breakfast. She frowned again. Gemma could be so unpredictable. Who on earth would have thought she would have leapt to the defence of Luke O'Rourke so determinedly, and all on the strength of one brief conversation?

He *was* very attractive of course, if one liked that type.

'Mother, Luke was simply being polite to me,' Gemma interrupted now, tired of the argument, 'not trying to get me into his bed.'

The minute the words were out, Gemma regretted them. In the background she could hear her mother's shocked denials, but she wasn't listening to them. Instead she was being overwhelmed by a mental image of Luke as she remembered him, his body hard and sleek as he came towards her from the river. He still had that same body now and it was all too easy for her to imagine it divested of its expensive clothes: flagrantly masculine, essentially male.

'Gemma, you're not listening to me at all.'

'I'm sorry, mother, I'm tired. Would you mind if I went to bed?'

What on earth had possessed her to conjure up that sort of vision of Luke? It was an intrusion into his personal life of the worst sort; a kind of voyeurism that angered and disgusted her.

It must have been the shock of seeing him, she decided as she went upstairs. That must have temporarily unbalanced her in some way.

CHAPTER FOUR

'THERE, that's the last of the place cards.'

Gemma smiled at Sophy across the desk in her father's study. Very wisely, in Gemma's view at least, her father and David had elected to make the day before the wedding a normal working one, which left her and Sophy, and Sophy's aunt, on hand at home to help her mother with any last-minute arrangements.

Any? Gemma grimaced to herself as her mother bustled in. 'Gemma, the place cards. They're waiting for them in the marquee.'

'They're all finished now—do you want me to take them across?'

'Would you, darling? I'm just on my way down to the church to check on the flowers. Sophy, you look exhausted, you poor child. Why don't you and your aunt go home for a while and rest? Gemma, what time did your uncle say they would arrive?'

'If you're talking about Uncle George and Aunt Letty, they should be here just before dinner, and before you ask I've already checked at the Rose and Crown and their rooms have been reserved.

'It's such a pity that the Lord Lieutenant won't be able to make it for dinner tonight, but they had a prior engagement. You haven't met Lord Chalmers yet, have you, Gemma? He is the most charming man.'

She was glad to escape from the house, even if it was

only a brief respite, Gemma reflected as she headed through the open french windows and across to where men in overalls were putting the finishing touches to the newly erected marquee.

Beneath her feet, the lawn glowed jewel-green, its surface perfectly smooth and completely unmarred by so much as a daisy. The men had arrived early in the morning and they had been working on the marquee all day.

Her mother was using the same company who had provided the marquees for the Duchess of Westminster's twenty-first birthday party and Gemma had reached the stage where she could feel herself gritting her teeth every time she heard her mother relate this small titbit of information to her friends and family. Why was it that these small snobbishnesses in her mother irritated her so much when in someone else she could have by-passed them with no more than a wry smile? When she had first announced to her parents that she wanted to teach in a socially deprived area, her father had accused her of deliberately turning her back on their way of life and all the advantages they had given her, but her feelings went far deeper than mere adolescent rebellion against the values and lifestyle of her family.

It had been Luke who had first opened her eyes to the harsh reality of poverty. He had been the one who had made her see that there were as many crippling inequalities in her own country as there were in those abroad that she saw and wondered at in news bulletins.

And now that she had experienced those inequalities for herself, she was even more revolted by them than she had been as a teenager. It was wrong that human beings should be cooped up in tall confining blocks of flats, in an environment that was alien and unnatural. Her own flat was luxurious compared to some of the ones occupied by her pupils and their families. No wonder their bleak environment bred in so many of her pupils their almost mindless sense of despair and ill-usage.

Until she had left home she hadn't really known what privilege was. Just to be able to look on this fresh, clean countryside. She sighed faintly to herself as she stepped into the marquee, and was immediately absorbed into the busy hubbub going on inside.

The sides of the tent had been hung with pink and white festooned silk, and at one end there was a raised dais for the band. Tables were being set out, that tomorrow morning would be covered with crisp white linen cloths; a carpet covered the floor, and some of the men were working on the dance floor that had been put down in front of the dais.

Baskets of flowers hung from the supporting tent poles, and concealed lighting had been placed behind the festooned silk. Gemma handed the cards over to the woman in charge of the catering arrangements and went back outside.

No doubt there were a dozen or more small tasks her mother would find her to do if she went back to the house, but suddenly she had had more than enough of wedding talk and preparations.

An odd restlessness filled her and, without being aware of where she was going, she walked through the small gate at the bottom of the garden and along the narrow footpath that led down to the river.

When she reached the clearing where she and Luke

used to meet, she recognised that she had intended to come here all along. It was remarkable how little it had changed; she saw that one or two more trees had been felled, presumably by accident rather than design, but otherwise the small glade was very much as she remembered it. She could even still see the tree trunk that she and Luke used to lean against whilst they talked. She studied it absently, suddenly irritated with herself for coming here. What had she expected to find? Luke?

She was confusing the boy he had been with the man he had become. He had said to her that he wasn't ashamed of his past or his beginnings, but he obviously felt no sentimental attachment to them. To them or to her? she asked herself sardonically, chilled by the sudden surge of pain twisting inside her.

Impatient with herself and her mood, Gemma turned away. What was the matter with her? Until her mother had mentioned his name she had scarcely given a thought to Luke during the last ten years. Angrily she hurried back down the river path. She should be pleased that he had made such a success of his life, instead of coming here and mooning over a time she could never now recapture.

Luckily her mother was still at the church when she returned and was unaware of her defection.

Gemma endured the family dinner party her parents had insisted on giving the night before the wedding with as good a grace as she could muster. Privately she thought Sophy would have benefited from a quiet evening alone with her fiancé, rather than being subjected to the full formality of a lengthy meal. It

struck Gemma as she looked at her that the other girl
looked pale and tired. There were dark circles under her
eyes, and she looked anything but bridal. Gemma's
mother on the other hand looked positively blooming.

'It's an absolutely perfect day for a wedding, isn't it?'
    Gemma was standing in the kitchen, drinking coffee
with her mother's daily, who had arrived earlier than
usual so that she could take over all the more mundane
household chores, leaving Gemma's mother free to
concentrate on the wedding.
    'She'll make a lovely bride, won't she? So pretty and
blonde ... I'd have thought you'd have been a
bridesmaid.'
    Gemma was aware of the older woman's urgent
curiosity, but she refused to satisfy it, saying lightly
instead, 'I'd have looked silly, Mrs Briggs. I'd have been
towering over Sophy, and besides little bridesmaids
always look very sweet.'
    God, she was sounding just like her mother, Gemma
reflected grimly. But at least she had been successful in
diverting Mrs Briggs. She had started to tell Gemma
about all the weddings she had attended, animadverting
on the rival benefits of large or small bridal attendants.
After ten minutes, Gemma's mind went into automatic
shut-off. She poured herself a second cup of coffee, and
then escaped with her mother's breakfast tray.
    This morning her mother was having breakfast in
bed, and then the hairdresser would be arriving to do her
hair. Once that was done there would have to be the final
tour of the house and the marquee. Then the caterers
would arrive. Gemma almost groaned as she thought of

everything that would have to be endured before her brother finally became a married man.

David was coming down the stairs as she went up them. 'I'm just going down to the Rose and Crown to check that all the overnighters arrived safely. Tell you what, why don't you come with me?'

Leaving *her* to do all the checking while he sneaked off into the bar, Gemma thought sardonically.

'I can't, I'm afraid, David. Mother's already got me marked down for half a dozen more jobs here.'

'Just wait until it's your turn.'

If it ever was, she wasn't going to get married like this. She wanted a much quieter affair, preferably just the man she was going to marry and the necessary witnesses. She would like a church ceremony, though. First she would have to find the right man.

If she ever did, what would he make of her virgin state? Virginity had gone out of fashion, and she was uneasily aware of what an encumbrance hers would seem if she ever did fall in love; and then, unbidden and unwanted, the memory of Luke saying softly to her, "and it wasn't just how to kiss that I wanted to teach you", slid treacherously into her mind and she knew that if he had taught her how to make love she would have received that tuition from the hands of an expert. Even then, at twenty, he had had an aura of sexual expertise about him, even if she could only recognise it with hindsight. And why not? Luke was a supremely male animal and a very sexual one. She very much doubted that *he* had been alone when she had gone home to her chaste bed after the evenings they had spent together.

Luke ... Luke. Why on earth was she wasting so much time thinking about him? She would be far better employed worrying about how on earth she was going to get a congenial new job.

There was nothing she could do about that here, she admitted to herself. Jobs in teaching were getting scarcer. The cutbacks were affecting everyone.

The wedding took place on schedule at noon. After the ceremony and the photographs, the guests made their way to their seats inside the marquee.

Gemma, who had been kept busy by her mother, either being re-introduced to old friends of the family, or running small errands, gave a faint sigh of relief, thankful that she wasn't sitting on the top table.

As she stepped to one side to avoid bumping into one of the small page boys, whose satin knee pants were already ominously marked with grass stains, she collided with one of the other guests.

Firm hands steadied her, a vaguely familiar voice exclaiming pleasurably, 'Good heavens, it's Gemma, isn't it?' And she turned to discover that her saviour was none other than Tom Hardman.

'Tom!' She had no need to fake her delight as he kissed her soundly on one cheek. 'How lovely to see you.'

She knew that David had kept up their school friendship, but it hadn't occurred to her that Tom would be one of the guests. He wasn't much taller than she was herself and the bright fairness of his hair had faded to a warm brown, but he was still a very attractive man, she recognised, as his eyes crinkled teasingly.

'David did ask me to be one of his groomsmen but, unfortunately, I was tied up in business in the States and

I wasn't sure that I would be able to make it back in time. Luckily I did.'

Gemma couldn't help her mouth dimpling into a smile as she responded to the frankly flirtatious look in his eyes.

He was still holding her hand, and now he looked directly at both of them.

'No wedding or engagement rings. Does that mean what I hope it means?'

He was very direct and she liked that in him. She was also feminine enough to be pleased that she wasn't one of Sophy's bridesmaids and wearing the frilly confections of pale peach silk and bows that looked delightful on the four little girls that Sophy had chosen from among their combined small cousins. Instead, she was wearing a highly sophisticated and flattering silk suit that her mother had insisted on paying for.

Gemma had protested at first that she had plenty of things to wear and didn't need a new outfit that she could only wear once, but her mother had persevered and in the end Gemma had given in, making the proviso that the outfit must be one she could choose herself.

They had found it in Samuel Cooper's in Wilmslow, their nearest Cheshire town, and, although Gemma had protested that it was far too expensive, her mother had insisted that she could not attend her brother's wedding wearing an outfit that had been worn before.

Her suit was a three-piece really, in pure soft silk. It was French and cut as only the French know how to cut cloth. The skirt was dark grey and clung sleekly to her waist and hips, flaring gently past her knees. The jacket was vibrant yellow with grey revers, and the pretty spotted blouse that went underneath it was also grey and yellow. The shop had even been able to provide a matching hat in the same yellow, and Gemma knew without vanity that her outfit was one of the most elegantly expensive there.

'Are you here on your own?' Tom pressed, looking round as though half expecting a man to materialise possessively at her side.

'It looks very much like it. And you?' Gemma asked him.

'Very much so, I'm delighted to say. I suppose you'll be on the top table for the meal?'

Gemma shook her head. 'No, as a matter of fact . . .'

'Marvellous. Perhaps we could sit together.'

Gemma had done the place cards for her own table, and knew that Tom was not on it, so she shook her head.

'You must have been paired with someone. Why don't we swap the cards round? No one will know,' Tom wheedled outrageously.

Gemma laughed. He was wrong, her mother would know and she would be furious with Gemma for altering her carefully made arrangements. Gemma already knew that it was Luke who would be seated opposite her, so she shook her head again, more firmly this time.

'Very well then, but at least promise that you'll dance with me later?'

'I'd love to,' Gemma told him truthfully, glancing over her shoulder. 'I think we'd better go inside the marquee, otherwise we won't get anything to eat. I don't know about you, but I'm starving.'

As with everything else, her mother had paid careful attention to the wedding breakfast menu.

They were to start with asparagus, and then would come salmon soufflé served in a special cream sauce and accompanied by home-grown vegetables.

For sweet they were having tiny wild strawberries with cream, and if the guests did not realise that this simple little repast had cost an absolute fortune, then it would only be because they were not of sufficient social standing to appreciate what was being served to them.

Gemma was the last to arrive at her own table. From half-way across the marquee she was conscious of Luke monitoring her progress. Her Aunt Constance raised an interrogatory eyebrow at her as she reached her chair.

'Sorry I was delayed,' she apologised. 'I met an old friend.'

'Tom Hardman,' Luke interposed softly, watching her.

Gemma was surprised that he had recognised him, because she wasn't aware that Luke and Tom had ever met. For some reason she felt herself prickle defensively, as though somehow Luke was mocking the younger man.

'As a matter of fact it was,' she agreed stiffly.

'Smitten, was he?'

Gemma frowned across the table at him. Why on earth was Luke trying to goad her? 'I haven't the faintest idea,' she lied carelessly. 'We were just talking about old times.'

Luckily, before Luke could bait her any harder, the formalities of the wedding breakfast began.

After the meal, on her mother's instructions, Gemma started to circulate amongst the guests. Those who were either living or staying locally started to drift away for a brief respite and a change of clothes before the evening's festivities began.

Gemma was surprised to find herself alone with Luke, and even more surprised when he suggested that they went for a walk.

'Have you come to any decision about your job yet?' he asked her, taking her arm, and purposefully drawing her into a quieter part of the garden.

Gemma relaxed as she realised that he wasn't going to torment her about Tom.

'No, not really. I know I'm going to have to give in my notice, but apart from that ...' She shrugged fatalistically. 'Teaching jobs aren't that easy to come by these days.'

'Mm ... Well, I have a proposition I'd like to put to you.' They had reached the bottom of the garden, where the river path led through the fields and down to their old meeting place, and by mutual consent they started to walk along it.

'What sort of proposition?' She was frowning now, not really sure what Luke could mean.

'I'm looking for a new assistant,' he told her calmly, 'but only on a temporary basis, and I thought you might like the job. It would mean coming out to the Caribbean for a couple of months—the development out there has reached the stage where I want to keep an eye on it.'

Gemma was stunned.

'Your assistant ... but Luke, I haven't had the training for anything like that.'

He stopped abruptly and she almost cannoned into him. He had his back to the sun so that she couldn't see the expression on his face, but she could have sworn he was laughing at her as he said softly, 'Don't worry about that, I'll teach you all you need to know.'

She felt herself colour hotly, and was furious with both him and herself when he laughed. One cool finger lightly traced the path of the wave of colour that flooded up her throat and over her cheek.

'Luke, this is ridiculous,' she protested as she moved away. 'You can't possibly want me to work for you. I don't know the first thing about the construction industry.'

'Don't you?' he asked wryly. 'I seem to remember you know quite a lot about it. You're a very intelligent woman, Gemma. I need someone like that . . . someone I can trust. But of course if Hardman is back on the scene I can quite understand your reluctance to leave. After all, if you play your cards right there you might not even have to find another job. He comes from a very wealthy family, as I remember. Just the sort of husband material your parents would approve of.'

The mockery in his voice caught her on a vulnerable point, temper inflaming her eyes as she glared at him.

'I'm not looking for a husband, Luke, you already know that. And if I was . . .' Her hands clenched. 'If I was, I'd be looking for a man that I could love and respect, not someone who would suit my parents.'

He had moved slightly so that she could see him, and suddenly his lids dropped down over his eyes to conceal his expression from her.

'Yeah, just as long as he's got the right accent and comes from the right background.'

Gemma gritted her teeth against the hot denial burning in her throat. What right did Luke have to throw these insults at her? What had she ever done to give him the impression that her parents' opinions and way of life were important to her? She had thought that he knew her better, and it actually physically hurt that he should believe her to be cast in the same mould as her mother.

'If that's what you think of me, I'm surprised you want me as your assistant, Luke,' she told him tartly.

'It's because you are your parents' child, that I am asking you,' he responded, shocking her out of her anger. 'I'm a wealthy man now, Gemma, and having money brings its own burdens, as I've discovered. I'm getting a little tired of being pursued by dewy-eyed débutante types looking for a rich husband.'

He said it so bluntly that for a few moments she was totally confused. 'The Caribbean's awash with them,' he added curtly, 'and it will be part of your job as my assistant to keep them at bay.'

He saw the refusal forming in her eyes before she voiced it, and added softly, 'Another part of it will be to help me arrange an education programme for my labour force. A lot of them never got beyond high school, although it's not for lack of brains. School officially finishes at fourteen on most of the Caribbean islands, and further education can only be bought at a very costly price. I want to set up a system whereby any of my workforce who want to take advantage of it can attend evening classes. The development out there is going to take at least five years, and the way I see it the lessons will be an incentive to them to stay on.'

'What sort of lessons?'

'Mostly practical—engineering and construction

courses, with the necessary maths and science thrown in.'

'I'm not qualified to teach at those levels.'

'That won't be necessary. I don't want you to teach; I just want you to help me to set it up and perhaps find the right sort of courses and teachers.'

'But you said you only wanted a temporary assistant, for two months.'

'Frightened that you can't do it?' he taunted.

She knew that he was deliberately challenging her, but it made no difference. Before she could stop herself, Gemma said fiercely, 'No, I'm sure I can.' And then it was too late, and she saw from the gleam in Luke's eyes that he had her neatly trapped.

'There'll be other duties as well,' he warned her. 'You'll be my main liaison contact between the site and my office there. There'll be times when I won't be around to handle problems, and it will be up to you to use your own initiative. The technical team I have out there are the very best; you can rely on them completely. I don't use any underhand or cost-cutting methods on my sites, and everyone who works for me knows that. The safety limitations are always observed, and I come down pretty heavily on any of the men I find abusing them. I'm telling you this just so that you know how things are run out there. I don't go for graft or any other kind of illegal operation, so if you spot something that looks like one, you tell me about it.'

Why was he telling her this? She frowned. 'Do you have much trouble with that sort of thing?'

'Occasionally, which is why I like to have it checked at the outset. I'm not asking you to play private detective, don't think that, I just don't want you getting the wrong idea. I don't turn a blind eye to anything illegal on my sites, and so I don't expect you to do so, either.'

'It seems to me that I'm going to have a very busy two months,' Gemma said wryly. 'Where will you be when you're not on hand then? Screening the débutantes?'

His eyebrows rose, and she felt that her remark had been too acid, but all he said was, 'You're going to take the job, then?'

Was she? She had to admit that it sounded fascinating; a real challenge, the sort of thing that appealed immensely to her. Add to that two months in the Caribbean. How could she refuse?

But Gemma was by nature cautious, and so she said slowly instead, 'I'd like to think about it if you don't mind, Luke. It's a marvellous opportunity, but I want to check that I'll be up to it, do a little bit on the sort of courses you need to run, the availability of text books, etc.'

'You've got three days,' he told her curtly. 'At the end of the week I fly back to the Caribbean and if you take the job you'll be coming with me.'

'Where were you yesterday afternoon, by the way? I called round to talk to you about this then, but you were out.'

It never occurred to her to dissemble. 'I went for a walk, and ended up in our clearing.'

A curious look crossed his face. 'Sentimental of me, wasn't it?' she said lightly, not sure how to interpret his silence. 'Do you ever wish you could turn the clock back, Luke?'

She must be going insane. What on earth had made

her ask that? He looked at her for a moment and then said drily, 'Not if it means going back to take a bath in the river. These days I prefer a warm shower.'

Illuminatingly she had an appallingly clear picture of him emerging from the river, his skin streaked with water, brown and hard where it lay over his muscles. He would still look like that now. And although she hadn't known before that she had even been aware of it, she could suddenly recall the clean male scent of him and the feel of his skin beneath her hand.

'We'd better get back,' he told her abruptly. 'Otherwise Hardman might come looking for you.'

'There's no reason why he should.'

'Come off it, Gemma, he was looking at you this afternoon like a dog guarding a particularly juicy bone. Remember,' he told her when they reached the gate that opened into her parents' garden, 'you've got three days to make up your mind, that's all.'

Her father saw them coming up through the garden together and came over to them, detaching Luke and telling him that he had some friends he wanted him to meet.

'Your mother's been looking for you,' he told Gemma, frowning slightly as he added, 'Where have you been?'

'I've just been trying to persuade Gemma to give up her job and come and work for me,' Luke interposed carelessly.

No wonder her father looked shocked, Gemma reflected. She had been more than a little stunned herself.

'Work for *you*? But Gemma's a teacher.'

Economically and quickly Luke explained why he felt that Gemma could be of use to him.

'You're far too soft on your workers, Luke,' her father protested with a frown. 'You're spoiling them. The minute you educate them they'll turn on you and start demanding higher wages. It's the old story.'

'I don't think so. My workforce is already well paid. I believe in giving a man a fair day's wage for a fair day's work.'

'You're a revolutionary . . . do you know that?'

Gemma left them to it. Although his success meant that her father was forced to bow to Luke's view, she could see that he didn't wholly approve of what Luke was doing. As far as her father was concerned, an unbridgeable gap existed between himself and his workforce, and that was the way he preferred it to be.

Sophy was remaining in her wedding dress for the evening, but everyone else seemed to be getting changed. Her mother had wanted to buy Gemma a new ballgown, but she had reminded her that she still had the dress she had worn for her own twenty-first birthday and reluctantly her mother agreed that she could wear it.

Her mother still wanted to show her off, just as she had done when she was a little girl, Gemma thought wryly as she went upstairs to change. And just as she had when she was a child, she was prepared to pet and fuss her in public, but in private she knew that the alienation between them was still very strong. The problem was that she and her mother had so little in common.

The dress she had had for her twenty-first was made of soft apricot raw silk. It had off-the-shoulder sleeves and a tight bodice, with a full length bell-shaped skirt.

It hung a little loosely on her waist now because she had lost a little weight, but the apricot silk flattered her skin, and the light bodice showed off the feminine shape of her breasts.

She gathered her hair back in a soft knot, and tucked a silk flower attached to a comb into it.

She was the first one back downstairs. A maintenance firm was busily picking up debris from the lawns, returning them to their earlier pristine splendour ready for the returning evening guests. The band had arrived and Gemma could hear them tuning up through the open french windows.

'Ah, there you are, darling. Daddy won't be long.' Her mother patted delicately at her prettily made-up eyes with a handkerchief. 'I can hardly believe it: my little boy married.'

David and Sophy had retired to their own new house to prepare for the evening celebrations amid bawdy amusement from the younger guests.

Why on earth did this suggestive humour still cling to weddings? Gemma wondered. Surely there could be few couples these days who went to the altar sexually ignorant of one another?

'Daddy has just been telling me that Luke has offered you a job. Are you going to take it?'

'I don't know.'

'Well it's a wonderful opportunity for you, darling, two months in the Caribbean, but ...' Her mother twisted her rings round nervously. 'Well, Daddy and I think we ought to give you a little warning. Luke does have something of a reputation where women are concerned, you know, and we wouldn't want you . . .'

Her mother didn't want her to take the job, Gemma recognised. It was all right for her to pair her off with him here at home where she could keep an eye on them, but if Luke took her to the Caribbean . . .

'Oh, I think I'm safe enough from any advances from him, Mother,' Gemma said coolly. 'I hardly think I'm his type.'

She could see that her mother wanted to press the subject, as she smiled at her and said instead, 'I hadn't realised that Tom Hardman was going to be one of the guests.'

Immediately her mother fell for the red herring and started to expound at length on Tom's virtues.

CHAPTER FIVE

SHE might have soothed down her mother's fears, Gemma reflected half an hour later as she absently watched the dancers, but her own were still dangerously ruffled. She wasn't a child any more, for God's sake, and if she wanted to go and work for Luke then she damned well would.

It infuriated her that her mother couldn't see behind her petty snobbishness to the real world that lay beyond it. Her mother looked down on Luke because he 'wasn't one of us'. Gemma had precious little doubt that, had it been Tom who wanted to employ her, she would have been practically thrown into his arms.

Was it really the loss of her virtue that her mother feared, or the public coupling of her name with Luke's? Gemma was no fool; she was perfectly well aware that if she went to work for him there would be some gossip. In such a small village it was naïve to assume that there wouldn't be, but once she and Luke had gone the gossip would die down.

The more she dwelt on her mother's objections, the firmer became her conviction that she wanted to accept Luke's job offer. As always, she railed mentally against the narrowness of her mother's views, and her total lack of awareness of how obvious she made them to others.

She was still standing in a corner of the marquee watching the dancers when her father came over to join her.

Conversation between the two of them was nearly always fraught with constriction, but on this occasion she could see the frowning tension in her father's eyes even before he spoke.

'Your mother and I have just been discussing O'Rourke's suggestion that you work for him,' he began without preamble, his frown deepening as he watched the faintly betraying tightening of her mouth. 'Now look, Gemma, your mother and I have been very patient with you. Heaven knows you've caused enough gossip with this teaching thing . . . but this . . . I hope you told him that you won't accept the job.'

'As a matter of fact . . .' She was just about to tell her father that she hadn't considered it properly when he went on before she could speak.

'He's not one of us, you know, Gemma. And I'm afraid his reputation with women . . . well, quite frankly it's distinctly unsavoury.'

'Really? But that doesn't seem to have stopped you from wanting to go into business with him, or Mother from inviting him here to dine.'

She could see that she had annoyed her father. His face was slowly turning a dark puce, always a sign that he was about to lose his temper.

'As far as I'm concerned his affairs are his own concern. The type of women he takes up with seem to know what life's all about. I dare say they know he's a man who won't make any commitment to them, but I won't have my daughter put in the same class as them.'

'I think you're letting your imagination run away with you.' Gemma told him angrily. 'Luke has offered me a job, and that job does not include sharing his bed.'

She could see that she had shocked him, and inwardly

she was torn between tears and laughter. Her parents were so ridiculously old-fashioned. Of course people would gossip, but did they really believe that her supposed reputation was more at risk in Luke's company than it would have been had her employer been Tom, for instance? And did they also think that she was no more than a puppet doll, incapable of making her own decisions about her life? It was up to her who became her lover—only she could make that choice and only she would. Oh, good heavens! The whole thing was getting out of hand. Luke had offered her a job, not the position of *maîtresse en titre*!

'It's just not on, Gemma, and you'll have to tell him so. There's no need for you to have a job at all, you know. In fact, your mother could do with your help at home. You've always been a rebellious and difficult child. Why can't you be more like Marjorie Walters?'

Marjorie Walters was the daughter of her father's architect: a languid blonde, who lived in a converted garage flat adjoining her parents' house.

What would her father say if she told him that Marjorie had lost her virginity at the age of sixteen to her father's trainee assistant, and that since then there had been a succession of men through her life?

He wouldn't believe her, Gemma thought bitterly.

'Well, Gemma, do I have your promise that you will tell O'Rourke that you won't be accepting his offer?'

It took Gemma several seconds to control the rush of anger she could feel surging through her body.

With commendable calm she faced her father and said quietly, 'No, Father, I'm afraid you don't. You see, I have every intention of working for Luke, and I'm going to tell him so right away.'

She walked off before he could stop her, shocked to discover that she was literally shaking with rage. She would *not* have her life manipulated in this way. She would make her own decision, live her own way.

She was so blinded by anger that she almost walked right into Luke.

'Hey, what's the matter? Had a quarrel with the boyfriend?'

'Boyfriend? I don't have a boyfriend,' she said flatly, adding impatiently, 'Luke, I have to talk to you.'

'You're doing that.'

'No, not here. Somewhere more private.' She thought for a moment. 'The summerhouse. Come on.'

At any other time she would have been amused at her own presumption in expecting him to follow her. Even as a younger man, Luke had never been someone who could be ordered around.

The summerhouse was on the far side of the garden from the marquee. Octagonal and open on three sides, it was a copy of the pretty Chinese follies favoured during the Regency era.

Normally the wooden seats were covered in a Chinesey chintz-covered padded seat, but this had been put away by the gardener so that it wouldn't spoil with dew; Gemma was unaware of the hard dampness of the wooden seat as she sat down on it.

'All right, what's bugging you?'

'I've decided that I want to accept your job.'

She couldn't look at him, but kept her eyes fixed on her tensed curled hands.

'I thought you wanted time to consider things.'

She could tell that he was frowning and her heart suddenly leaped like a stranded fish. Had he changed his mind? Didn't he want her after all?

She said as much, and the cool amusement in his voice as he told her softly, 'Oh yes, I still want you,' drew her eyes to his face, but there was nothing she could read there to reinforce the faint twinge of disquiet the mocking words aroused.

'But why the sudden decision? Or can I guess? Had a quarrel with the boyfriend, have you?'

The boyfriend? Her forehead creased.

'Hardman,' he told her laconically. 'I saw you talking with him earlier. I'm not that naïve, Gemma. There has to be some reason for this oh, so sudden decision.'

No, he wasn't naïve, and if she denied that Tom was her boyfriend, he would keep on pressing her until he had the truth, and Gemma knew that no matter how much they might deserve it, she couldn't expose her parents' petty snobbery to him. It would be easier and simpler to let him believe that he was right and that Tom was the reason she had made up her mind so quickly.

'Does it matter what the reason is, as long as you have my decision?'

She could feel him watching her, and the sombreness of his regard made tiny prickles of sensation lift on her skin: not fear exactly, not excitement either, but something that was a combination of the two.

'Maybe not, but I warn you, now that you have given me your decision I won't allow you to back out. So I'll ask you again, are you sure?'

Was she? She had the sensation of stepping off the known and firm ground beneath her and on to something unknown, alien, and quite possibly dangerous, but she didn't hesitate.

'I want to come with you, Luke.'

'Very well.' He stood up, and she stood up with him. Even with her heels on he was still much taller than her, and much broader, too. He obviously didn't sit in an office all day long.

'Now, we'd better go back and join the others before your father comes looking for me with a shotgun.'

'You say that as though you're speaking from previous experience,' Gemma teased, striving to introduce a lighter note into their conversation.

'Maybe. Any man with money soon discovers that he's a target for females on the lookout for a meal ticket for life, and despite the progress of the women's movement there are still plenty about.'

'You don't want to get married then, Luke?'

'Why should I?' he drawled mockingly. 'You know what they say about marriage—and I did my share of living in an institution when I was a kid.'

For some reason she felt oddly depressed, although his remark was no more than she had expected. She couldn't really see Luke as a married man, tied down with a wife and children. He was too independent, too much an animal who walked alone. She wondered if he would ever allow anyone to get close enough to him to endanger that precious solitude.

They had walked through the trees and were now within sight of the marquee, but before she could move any further Gemma suddenly felt his hand on her arm constraining her.

As she turned to look at him, she saw the white flash of his smile illuminated by the moon.

'Not yet. We still have to seal our contract.'

'What contract? You haven't given me one yet.'

'Oh, yes, I have, and now you've accepted it—even if

it is only verbal. And, remember, I intend to keep you to it, Gemma. There was a time in the past when a kiss was a pledge, not so much of sexual desire, but of trust and loyalty.'

She had known all the time what he was leading up to and there had been ample opportunity for her to draw away, but somehow she couldn't; somehow she had remained standing still so that he was able to draw her fully within the circle of his arms, her eyes as mesmerised as a firefly caught in a bright light as she stood staring up at him, waiting for his hard, warm mouth to come down over hers, her body tense with nervous excitement.

It was just before his mouth claimed hers that she remembered how she had felt that first time he kissed her. Every detail of those few seconds came back to her as though they had happened only minutes before.

She felt his mouth move on hers, warm and sure, his tongue slowly probing at her closed lips until, unable to resist the delicious torment, they opened eagerly to his command.

He was straining her against his body now, and she was helping him, enjoying the electric tension in her breasts as they pressed against the hard wall of his chest. Even through his evening jacket she could feel the heavy thud of his heart. His hands slid slowly down her back, cupping her gently and easing her against the hardness of his thighs, while his mouth continued to coax and seduce hers into eager surrender.

She had never been kissed like this before, had never felt this mindless urge to respond, to lose herself completely in the heat and hardness of the male body dominating her own.

She had never dreamed it was possible to be so aroused by a mere kiss, and the instant she realised how aroused she was she tensed in shock, reality pouring over her body like iced water.

'I thought we were making a pledge,' she complained huskily when she had her voice sufficiently under control. She would die if he said anything to her about her abandoned response. Even now her skin still tingled, and her lips felt swollen and soft. She couldn't look at him properly because if she did ... if she did she would want to be back in his arms. The knowledge stunned her. What had happened to her? She and Luke had always been good friends, but she had never really had any sexual feelings for him. And she didn't have now, she told herself. Her feelings were simply reaction, a blend of the anger she had felt towards her parents, and the ambience of being alone in a summer garden with a very attractive and sensual man.

'We were,' Luke told her softly in answer to her question, and although there was nothing remotely desirous in his eyes, Gemma still felt something vulnerable and feminine tremble nervously deep inside her, as though somehow he had staked a claim on that part of her that had always remained inviolate and unawakened.

'We'd better go and join the others before they send out a search party.' She tried to sound brisk and matter of fact but she knew her voice was far from controlled.

As luck would have it, her father and Tom were talking right outside the entrance to the marquee.

Tom frowned when he saw them approach.

'I've been looking for you, Gemma,' he complained. 'You promised me a dance.'

'Luke and I . . .'

'Have been finalising the details of Gemma's employment with me,' Luke interrupted smoothly. 'She's coming to work for me as my personal assistant.'

Gemma could feel her father's anger, although he made no comment. He wouldn't want to offend Luke, Gemma recognised, so he would keep his feelings to himself. He would not dare to say to Luke the things he had said to her.

Tom was looking equally shocked. 'I thought you were working on a project in the Caribbean at the moment.'

'I am,' Luke agreed blandly, and Gemma had the feeling that Luke was both amused and contemptuous of Tom's startled reaction. But then he would be if he thought that she and Tom were far more than mere acquaintances, she realised, remembering their conversation.

'I thought you wanted to dance with me,' she reminded Tom, leaving Luke's side to slip her arm through the younger man's.

She was glad that there wasn't going to be a long delay before they left the country. She suspected that her father was not going to make life easy for her in the intervening period.

She danced with Tom for almost half an hour. Their steps matched well and she enjoyed his company. He made her laugh with his droll self-mockery and she found herself wishing that she had made his reacquaintance earlier. Still, her job with Luke was only a temporary one, and there would be plenty of time to pick up the threads of her old life once she got back. Even so, she found it rather disquieting to admit how much her father's pompous attitude had had to do with her rash decision to accept Luke's offer.

On the face of it, working in the Caribbean sounded idyllic, but would she be able to cope with the tasks that Luke had outlined? She sensed that he would expect others to perform to the same high standards he had achieved himself, and she honestly didn't know if she was up to it. And then there was Luke himself. She missed a step and apologised to Tom, seeing his frown as she said lightly, 'I'm sorry, I was miles away.'

'Thinking about O'Rourke, I suppose.'

She was astounded by Tom's percipience, and said before she could stop herself, 'How did you know?'

'Instinct, I suspect. You'll be careful while you're working for him, won't you, Gemma?' He saw her face and added hastily, 'Look, I'm sorry, I shouldn't have said that. It's none of my business, but your father . . .'

'Father is afraid that people will gossip. He doesn't want his daughter's name connected with that of a man who isn't one of our small social circle,' Gemma said bitterly.

'Well, you have to admit that O'Rourke is something of an unknown quantity. I have my own selfish reasons for wishing you weren't going . . .'

His hand tightened momentarily on hers and Gemma smiled up at him, then for some reason she felt compelled to glance across the marquee. Almost immediately her glance clashed with Luke's. He was watching them with an odd expression of his face. A mixture of contempt . . . and what? Gemma felt her heart pound heavily as, inexplicably, she was reminded of the feeling of his mouth on hers, and of the way she had responded.

'I suspect that few women would be immune to him if

he chose to charm them,' Tom continued gloomily. 'He doesn't fit into any pre-ordained mould, does he? He's an outlaw to the rules that govern the rest of us; there's something restless and dangerous about him. Women seem to find that a fascinating mixture.'

'I'm going to be working for him, Tom, nothing else,' Gemma pointed out gently.

'Good ... And when you come back, I want you to come out with me.'

'When I come back, perhaps I will.'

'It looks like David and Sophy are leaving,' Tom told her. 'We'd better go over and say our goodbyes.'

Gemma hadn't been aware of her brother and new sister-in-law disappearing to change into their travelling clothes, but now she went forwards with Tom to kiss and hug Sophy and to tease her brother on his new status as a married man.

Her mother, needless to say, was weeping prettily into a diminutive lacy handkerchief. She kissed Sophy with real affection and joy, and Gemma knew that she would have much more pleasure in her daughter-in-law than she had ever had in her daughter.

She doubted that David and Sophy would waste much time in starting a family. Her parents would be adoring and doting grandparents. Sighing faintly, Gemma moved to one side to allow the bridal couple room to leave the marquee.

Almost directly across from her she could see Luke. Clinging to his arm was Marjorie Walters. The other girl was simpering up at him, pressing herself against his arm so that her generous breasts were in danger of completely spilling over the brief top of her gown. Marjorie had blond hair and huge blue eyes. Privately

Gemma had always felt vaguely sorry for her, pitying her apparently constant need for company in her bed.

She had been married briefly, but had claimed that her husband beat her, and the marriage had been set aside. Personally Gemma had thought its failure owed more to the fact that her new husband hadn't been able to support Marjorie in the style to which her father had accustomed her than to anything else, and this slightly bitchy reflection was very much to the forefront of her mind now as she watched Marjorie's kittenish antics with Luke.

Sophy was still clutching her bouquet, and when she tossed it in her direction Gemma caught it automatically, only realising the significance of her actions when everyone around her started to clap and laugh. Her mother of course was delighted; she was positively simpering at Tom, Gemma realised, gritting her teeth. Aware of the obvious speculation she could sense all around her, her unwary gaze became trapped by Luke's as she glanced angrily away from her mother.

Luke wasn't sharing in the good-humoured amusement of the others. He was frowning, apparently unaware of Marjorie clinging so determinedly to his arm.

Would he be sharing the big double bed in the flat over the garage tonight? Gemma wondered. Possibly not. She suspected that Luke was the kind of man who preferred to take his women to his own bed, rather than to share theirs. Where *was* he staying? At the village pub, presumably although she now remembered her father saying something about him having offices in Chester. Perhaps he also had a home there.

It was rather odd, surely, that such a large construction company as the one Luke had built up should have offices in a small place like Chester. Wouldn't London have been the more obvious choice?

'This looks to me very much like a good omen,' Tom whispered in her ear, distracting her, as he touched the bouquet she was holding.

For some reason his pretty compliment irritated her. Luke would never have used such an obvious ploy; she only had to look at his sardonic expression now to know that.

'I think it was more of a carefully planned manoeuvre on the part of my mother,' Gemma told him drily. 'She's beginning to think that I'm going to be left on the shelf.'

That was a mistake, because Tom immediately started to reassure her that nothing was further from the case. She liked him, and he could be good fun—as a friend. The very fact that she could make such a qualification on so short an acquaintance puzzled her. It was almost as though she already knew the type of man she could love and that, having known him, no one else could come anywhere near to matching his image, which was ridiculous because she had never been in love, never found anyone with whom, she would want to spend the rest of her life. Good grief, Luke was the only man who had ever managed to stir her to passion; that was how ignorant of sexual desire she was.

Once the bridal couple had left, the party started to break up. Even so, it was gone three o'clock in the morning before Gemma finally managed to get to bed.

The following day, those members of the family who were staying in the village were expected to lunch, but Gemma made her excuses and escaped as soon after this meal as she could.

It had been a rather strained occasion for her. Her father was very obviously furious with her while her mother was still feeling weepy and inclined to verbally lament her only daughter's wilful stubbornness.

It was not an atmosphere that Gemma could endure for very long without exploding, so she took herself off down along the river path, pausing once to watch two otters at play, and then again when she saw a mother moorhen leading her growing brood of chicks from one river bank to the other.

It was another perfect day; the sun seemed almost to hang motionless in the sky, and all around her the fields were heavy with their crops.

There was something about Cheshire that was quintessentially English: black and white timber and plaster farmhouses; gently rolling countryside bordered by purple-hazed mountains; the broad, smooth-flowing river, so clear that she could see the pebbles on the bottom and the shadows of its fish. Without the slightest effort at all, it was easy to imagine oneself back in time to a different England. Not very far away from here was historic Gawsworth, with its sombre pools and its macabre story of Shakespeare's wanton lovely Mary, who had, so it was said, thrown herself into one of them rather than endure her disgrace.

Had either of her famous lovers truly mourned her passing? Shakespeare had loved her and written about her in his sonnets, and Southampton had seduced her, but she was the one who had suffered. It was nearly always women who suffered for their love, Gemma recognised, shivering slightly, and rubbing the resultant gooseflesh from her arms. What was the matter with her today? She wasn't normally so introspective.

Almost without intending to, she walked as far as her old meeting place with Luke.

Finding an old tree stump to sit down on, she tried to sort out her confused thoughts. Did she really want to work for him, to leave everthing that was familiar, or had she simply acted out of anger, driven to accept the job because of her father's stubborn narrow-mindedness? She moved uncomfortably on her makeshift seat, remembering how often as a child she had been criticised for being impulsive. Nothing had changed; she was still inclined to act first and think afterwards.

'You're looking very pensive.'

'Luke!' She sprang up at the sound of his voice and whirled round to find him leaning against a tree not five yards away, studying her. 'I didn't hear you.'

'You were so deep in thought you wouldn't have heard a charging buffalo,' he told her drily. 'And I suspect I don't need a crystal ball to guess what about. I warned you last night, Gemma, that I wouldn't let you back out of our agreement.'

'How did you know I was here?' She felt thoroughly confused now, thrown off course by his unexpected appearance.

'I didn't.' He was watching her with what she could only describe as a very guarded expression.

'Then why come here?'

He smiled sardonically. 'Why not?'

He was quite right, of course. Why shouldn't he come here, and why should she automatically suppose that, because he had, it meant he was looking for her?

'However, since you *are* here, I hope your passport is up to date, Gemma. I want to fly out to the island on Saturday.'

It was. She had obtained a ten-year passport three years previously for a continental holiday.

'I'd also like you to come to Chester and sign the contract my people are drawing up. It should be ready by tomorrow morning.'

'My goodness, you *have* been busy. I'm surprised that Marjorie let you out of her sight long enough for you to be in touch with your office.'

She knew that the remark was bitchy but she hadn't been able to keep it back. To her relief, although his eyebrows rose slightly, Luke didn't seem disposed to take offence. In fact he appeared to be slightly amused rather than anything else.

'Dear me,' he mocked, shattering her self-confidence both with the tone of his voice and the way he looked at her. 'Am I to take it from that that *your* night wasn't similarly pleasantly occupied? Don't worry about it. I'm sure it was only because Hardman is far too much of a gentleman to make love to you beneath your parents' roof.'

'A reticence you don't seem to share,' Gemma snapped waspishly.

'In regard to you, or in regard to Marjorie?' Luke countered with devastating smoothness. 'If we're talking about the latter, you're quite right of course, but on this occasion you're wrong.'

Which left her no closer to knowing whether or not he had spent the night with Marjorie, Gemma thought in bitter frustration. Only why should she want to know? She stood stock still, staring at him with huge shocked eyes, and then swallowed nervously. What was the matter with her? It was no concern of hers who Luke did or did not sleep with.

'When do you want me to come to your office?' she asked him huskily.

'Tomorrow morning, if that's convenient. I'd offer you lunch but I have several appointments taking up most of the day, I'm afraid.'

'That's all right. I ... I have several things to do myself.' Nothing that couldn't have been put off, but she didn't want Luke to think that she had expected him to take her for lunch, or that she even wanted his company. Because she didn't. She was no Marjorie, constantly on the look out for a man to give her pleasure.

She glanced at her watch. 'I ought to be getting back.'

His smile mocked her, although she didn't know why. It was almost as though he knew something about her that she didn't know about herself. She should never have made that remark about Marjorie, she recognised, as she reached the sanctuary of her parent's garden; she had no right at all to betray the slightest degree of curiosity about his sex life. No right at all.

CHAPTER SIX

FIVE days later when Gemma stood beside Luke in the departure lounge at Heathrow Airport, Marjorie, and all of her own doubts about the wisdom of accepting Luke's job offer, were pushed to the back of her mind, and all Gemma could think of was the excitement of her new life.

The Caribbean would be a completely new experience for her. She and Luke had travelled down to Heathrow together the previous morning and they had stayed overnight at the conveniently placed Holiday Inn, in order to be fresh and on time for the early morning flight to St George's.

On the journey down and over dinner the previous evening Luke had gone into greater detail about his Caribbean venture, and Gemma had learned that he was constructing a holiday complex similar to the one owned by Peter de Savary on Antigua. When Gemma had queried the market for two such upmarket holiday complexes, Luke had assured her that the business was definitely there. 'Some of the villas we are constructing will be sold outright, others will be operated under a "time share" scheme, and ownership of some will be retained by one of my companies and they'll be let out on a rental basis.'

In addition to the luxurious villas and apartments, the complex was to include a golf course, tennis courts, several swimming pools, bars, restaurants, a marina, a select parade of shops; in fact, every conceivable luxury the holidaymakers could want.

'At the moment we're only in the very initial stages,' Luke told her, going on to warn her, 'and one building site is very much like another, whether it's in Cheshire or the Caribbean, so don't expect too much. Luckily the land I purchased already included its own small harbour and beach.'

'It sounds idyllic, but it must have cost the earth, surely? Enough land for the sort of develpment you're planning must be in great demand.'

'It is,' Luke agreed, 'but I just dropped lucky. The previous owner, a man in his late seventies, was slightly eccentric in that he had his own views on how he wanted the land to be used and how he believed the local population should be treated. Luckily for me they happened to coincide with mine. I met him quite by chance while I was on holiday over there—it was only after that I learned about his land. When the time came for him to sell, he actually approached me.'

'Who will run the venture once it's completed?' Gemma had asked him. 'Will you move out there yourself permanently?'

Luke had shook his head. 'No, the lotus-eating life isn't for me. I like St George's, but only in short doses. I'll appoint a manager to take charge of the complex when it's eventually finished, but I want to retain as much local labour as possible, and that's one of the reasons why I want to provide educational facilities for my workers.'

Gemma had spent almost two full days tracking down various educational courses she thought might be applicable. She had also priced up the books and equipment that would be needed, and scribbled down tentative notes on how the course she had chosen could be tailored to fit in with Luke's requirements.

'Postal HNC courses seem to come closest to what you have in mind,' she had told Luke the previous evening, and now, briefly, her excitement was subdued by a twinge of apprehension. What if she found the task Luke had given her was beyond her capabilities? What if . . .

Luke touched her arm. 'Come on, they've just called our flight for the second time.'

Nervously Gemma picked up her hand luggage and followed him towards the flight departure gate.

On Luke's advice she had kept separate from the rest of her luggage a change of clothes in lightweight cotton, plus her toilet things, so that she could freshen up and change in flight if she wanted to. She had elected to travel in a cool white cotton tracksuit, that was both attractive and comfortable. The top would be pleasantly warm in the air-conditioned cabin, and the trousers were in a modern style, cut off half-way past her knees.

Fortunately she already had the beginnings of a pretty tan from the week of good weather she had enjoyed at home. White canvas casual shoes with a blocked heel showed off the bright red polish she had applied to her toenails in a mood of bravado, and she had deliberately kept her make-up to a minimum.

Her casual taupe canvas bag was roomy enough to hold her change of clothes, plus her toilet requirements, and a couple of paperback books, and the wallet containing her passport, money and other documents. The flight was going to be a long one, at least seven hours, and Luke would expect her to keep herself entertained.

They were travelling first-class, and she was aware of the smiling looks the stewardesses gave Luke as they were shown aboard. Gemma had no preference for a window seat but, seeing that the aisle seat would give Luke a little more room to move his legs, when he offered her a choice, she slid into the seat by the window.

It had been several years since she had last flown and she was amazed by the speed with which they became airborne. After a very few minutes the stewardesses came round with menus for breakfast and, since she had only managed to eat half a slice of toast and drink a cup of coffee at the hotel, Gemma found that she was surprisingly hungry.

Like her, Luke was dressed casually, and, as she waited for the stewardess to bring their breakfast, Gemma cast a surreptitious look at him. He was wearing a pair of much-washed and faded denim jeans that hugged the lean contours of his body. The blouson cotton jacket he had been wearing when they came on board was now folded in the coat store above their heads, and through the fine checked cotton of his shirt Gemma could see the dark shadowing of hair on his chest.

Heat prickled through her quite unexpectedly and she withdrew her attention in some disarray, feeling her face suddenly start to burn. It was a most disconcerting reaction and one that wasn't in the slightest degree merited. Confused and rather dismayed, she glanced down at the floor.

'Are you all right?'

The light pressure of fingers on her arm, the controlled concern in his voice as Luke bent his head discreetly towards her, reminded Gemma of just how dangerously observant he could be.

'Yes . . . yes, I'm fine.'

'I thought for a moment you were feeling sick.'

Forcing a smile, Gemma looked up and across at him. Had he really thought that, or had he been aware of the way she had been watching him? He hadn't seemed to notice—but he had been quick to ask her if she was all right.

Fortunately he didn't seem disposed to press the point, which was just as well. She wasn't sure how she would have been able to explain to him that her tension had sprung from the fact that she had, quite devastatingly, realised what a physically compelling man he was.

At least, that wasn't entirely true. She had always realised it, but previously her knowledge had been tempered by a very large degree of detachment—until he had kissed her at the wedding, she reminded herself wryly. She had known that Luke was extraordinarily sexually attractive, but in the past had been relatively immune to that attraction, whereas now . . .

Her heart suddenly seemed to seize up in her chest; for a moment she actually thought she might stop breathing. So intense was her fit of panic that her heart started to pound; she dragged in a deep lungful of air, and her panic receded.

It must be something to do with the altitude, she told herself desperately. It couldn't possibly be Luke who was having this incredible effect on her. After all, she knew Luke. She knew that he wasn't a man who was interested in any form of permanent commitment.

Permanent commitment? What on earth was she thinking? she asked herself in self-disgust. All this heart-searching just because of a kiss and a tantalisingly shadowed glimpse of a male chest. What was she? Some sort of Victorian heroine?

Luckily the arrival of her breakfast precluded her from following this depressing avenue of reasoning.

To her chagrin, she found she could only toy with the breakfast she had ordered with such childishly greedy anticipation, while to her left Luke tucked into his with every evidence of enjoyment. Trying to give her thoughts a new direction, she made herself go over the events of the previous days. They had been so rushed that she still had the feeling that she had been picked up by an express train.

True to his word, Luke had had a contract of employment ready for her when she visited his Chester head office. She had telephoned the headmaster explaining the situation to him, and, as she had suspected he would be, he had been so delighted to hear that she was going to be amenable to his plans that he had readily agreed to waive the normal period of notice. He had met her at the school one afternoon, when she went to collect her things.

It hadn't taken her long, and despite its grimness she had started to walk away from it with a feeling of inner dissatisfaction for a job not finished. During holiday time the school grounds were made available, under supervision, for the pupils' use, and on her way to her car she had come across a group of her own form.

One of them had addressed her with a cheeky grin, and she had stopped to talk to them. She had asked them how they intended to spend the holidays, and had been overwhelmed with a feeling of helpless anger and compassion as she listened to their bored young voices.

What was there for them to do, living as they did on the outskirts of the city? There was no park for them to

play in, no cheap means of transport to take them out
into the country where they might have been able to run
off some of their surplus energy.

As she listened to them she had sensed within them
their own feeling of hopelessness, a feeling they tried
unsuccessfully to put into words.

Tommy Johnson came closest to describing their
feelings when he had complained angrily that there was
nothing for them to do. He had looked at her with
resentment and misery in his eyes, Gemma remembered, and there had been nothing she could say or do,
no consolation she could honestly offer them.

When they went back to school after the summer
break and found her gone, they would write her off as
yet another adult who had deserted them, not knowing
or understanding that she, like them, did not have free
choice.

She had ached with pity for them and anger for
herself. It was all so wrong, but what could she do? She
had stayed with them for half an hour or so, chatting to
them, but despite the rapport she had established with
them in class, she sensed that they were anxious for her
to be gone. She was not of their world, she realised,
sighing for all her own impossible plans and for the
grimness of their future.

That last final glimpse of them huddled together
against the dark backdrop of the school was one she
would carry with her for a long time.

Her father and mother were still none too pleased by
her decision of course, especially her father, and since he
would not quarrel with Luke, he was taking his ire out
on Gemma herself.

She felt guilty about how pleased she had been to get

away from home, but she mustn't forget that this job was merely a brief respite, she warned herself now, as the stewardess removed her half-eaten breakfast and poured her a fresh cup of coffee. When it was over, she would still be faced with the task of finding herself a new job. Time to worry about that when *this* job was over, Gemma told herself firmly, drinking the reviving brew, and trying to banish the sullen, hopeless expressions of her late pupils from her mind.

'If you're at all inclined to do so, I suggest that you try to have a nap,' Luke suggested at her side. 'It's the best way of passing the time on these tediously long flights.'

She had been right in thinking that Luke wouldn't want to be bothered with entertaining her, Gemma thought wryly, correctly interpreting his hint as he bent down to retrieve the folder of papers he had placed beneath his seat.

'I've brought a book with me,' Gemma told him, taking it out of her bag, 'so I won't disturb you if you want to work.'

She was as good as her word. The book was by one of her favourite writers, Catherine Gaskin, and she soon found herself so deeply involved in its story that not even Luke could break through its spell.

In the end he was the one who broke their companionable silence, grimacing faintly as he asked her, 'Do you want any lunch? They'll be coming round soon with the menus.'

Gemma could hardly believe so much time had passed. She closed her book with a faint sigh of regret, and turned to face him.

Surely that wasn't pique she saw in his eyes? What had he expected? she wondered, as she decided that it was. Had he thought that despite her promise she would try to engage him in conversation? A mischievious smile twinkled in her eyes. She suspected that it wasn't very often that anyone got the better of Luke O'Rourke, and the fact that she had done so in all innocence made it seem even funnier.

'Something amusing you?'

Gemma didn't quite like the glint in his eyes.

'No, nothing at all,' she fibbed smoothly. 'Did you get much work done?'

'Enough. I just wanted to recap on the reports from the construction site. You know, I'd forgotten how totally you can get absorbed in a book; for a time there I suspect you'd forgotten everything but what was happening here.' He tapped the book as he spoke, and Gemma smiled her agreement, unable to resist adding teasingly, 'But at least it kept me quiet, didn't it?'

His own expression ruefully acknowledged her point, and she added chidingly, 'Not all women chatter away like magpies, you know, Luke.'

'Maybe not, but they all have their own ways of attracting attention.'

Did that mean that he *had* expected her to try and distract him? The same faint unease she had experienced before touched her in a light *frisson*. Why should Luke expect her to want to distract him? Theirs was a business relationship, nothing more. Had she been male, he would not have expected her to demand that he give his attention to her and not to his work. Did he fear that she might try to trade on their old friendship? But if that was the case, why had he offered her the job in the first place? Through a mistaken sense of pity? She hoped not.

'Luke . . .' she began uncertainly, but he cut her off as the stewardess came up with the menus, and by the time they had chosen their lunch, Luke was discussing certain aspects of his plans for the complex with her, and she had lost both the opportunity and the impetus to question him more closely on his motives for bringing her to the Caribbean.

It was dusk when they eventually landed, the tropical moist dusk of the Equator, the sun a dying ball of fire in a sea of molten copper.

Gemma held her breath at the panoramic beauty spread out below her as the plane swept in a controlled arc out over the sea and then down towards the landing strip.

The heat muffled her like a warm damp blanket, and even though she thought she had been prepared for it, its intensity still almost smothered her. She could feel herself almost visibly wilting as she stood in the concrete arrivals hall, lulled into a state half-way between sleeping and waking by the rhythmic sound of the huge ceiling fans.

'Here, you'd better let me hold that.'

Before she could stop him, Luke had relieved her of both her passport and her hand luggage. She made a token protest, but felt too sleepy to do any more. The heat was so enervating. How on earth could she ever work in it?

'You'll soon get acclimatised, don't worry about it,' Luke murmured in her ear as they went through customs and she realised that she had voiced her doubts out loud.

A grinning porter—he couldn't be more than twelve years old, Gemma reflected, smiling a little at the boy's toughened bare feet and straw-hat-shaded face—wheeled their luggage triumphantly out to the waiting vehicle.

Luke had already mentioned that transport on the island was limited, and that on the construction site they used either Land Rovers or, in an emergency, hired some of the island's many beach buggies.

This was saffron yellow outside and in, a colour that couldn't have been better chosen to complement the colouring of the girl sitting in the driver's seat, one long leg dangling negligently over her door as she leaned back, listening to the reggae music pounding out of the cassette system. Her long dark hair was caught back in a yellow band the same colour as the buggy. Like the porter's, her feet were bare, but they weren't dusty as his had been, and her toenails were painted a vivid burnt orange to complement her stunning tan.

As Luke tapped her on the shoulder, she climbed languidly out of the car and threw herself into his arms.

She was tall, tall and very slim, and wearing the briefest pair of shorts Gemma had ever seen in her life. Like the band in her hair they were saffron yellow, matching the T-shirt she was wearing underneath a soft denim blue oversized sweatshirt that hung off one tanned shoulder and somehow emphasised the femininity of her slender body.

Gemma felt exceedingly *de trop* as she watched the other girl enthusiastically kissing Luke. *She* obviously didn't need any lessons, was her first, rather acid thought, and Luke certainly didn't seem to have any objections to the mode of greeting—but then, what man with red blood in his veins would?

At last he managed to disentangle himself and,

holding her at arm's length, he drawled, 'Surprise, surprise!'

'Oh, when Boyd told me you were coming in on this flight, I told him I'd come and pick you up. If we hurry we can just make it in time for dinner.'

'Sorry.' Luke's voice was decisively firm as he shook his head. 'Not tonight, I'm afraid, Josephine.' With one long arm he reached behind him to draw Gemma forward, making her suddenly acutely conscious of the fact that he had known exactly where she was, because he hadn't even had to turn round.

'Samantha—Gemma. Samantha's uncle is Larry Freman—the man I was telling you about. The man who sold me the land for the complex.'

'Darling, you didn't say you were bringing anyone back with you.'

Cold and rather hard brown eyes surveyed Gemma with icy disdain. Samantha was quite plainly not at all pleased at her presence.

'Gemma is here to work for me,' Luke responded, and Gemma could see from the narrowed speculation in Samantha's eyes that she was being warned off.

'Oh, I see,' she murmured indifferently, ignoring Gemma to smile ravishingly at Luke. 'She's one of your employees.'

'And a very old friend.'

Now why on earth had he said that? Gemma wondered in bewildered vexation. It must surely be obvious to him that it was the very last thing Samantha wanted to hear. It was patently obvious that the pair of them had been and possibly still were lovers, and, by claiming Gemma as an old friend, he had quite deliberately stirred up the other woman's jealousy.

Of course it could be that he wanted to make her jealous, but she wasn't going to be used as a pawn in that sort of game, Gemma thought angrily, trying to ignore the sharp sensation of pain clawing at her insides. Samantha wasn't the only one who was jealous, regrettably. All at once all her anticipation and excitement vanished, leaving her feeling tired and irritated. She wanted to get out of this muggy heat, to have a bath and lie down. She wanted . . . She wanted to be at home, she realised wryly. She wanted the security of the known, rather than the unfamiliarity of this alien island and this equally alien young woman.

'Really?' It wasn't a smile that Samantha gave her, more a baring of her perfect white teeth, Gemma thought, responding in kind.

'I'm afraid you're going to be rather squashed up in the back with all the luggage,' Samantha tossed carelessly over her shoulder in Gemma's direction as she slid her arm through Luke's and drew him slightly away, 'but then Luke never told us he was bringing . . . an old friend back with him.'

Us? That sounded very cosy and proprietorial, but what exactly did it mean?

'Uncle Larry's been missing his games of chess while you've been away, darling,' she cooed at Luke, completely ignoring Gemma.

Luke, it seemed, was equally oblivious to her presence, and a sudden surge of anger rocketed through her, taking her off guard, as she glared at his back. How dared he let this . . . this woman behave like this! How dared he bring her here and then leave her standing out in this appalling heat while he flirted with his girlfriend. She opened her mouth to tell him that she had changed her mind and that she wanted to go home, when suddenly he disengaged himself from Samantha and turned round.

'I think on this occasion you can sit in the back, Samantha. I'll drive and Gemma can sit beside me. That way I'll be able to make sure that she stays awake.'

Gemma wasn't sure which of them was the more stunned. Samantha certainly recovered first, shooting Gemma a look of bitter venom, but not arguing with Luke as she clambered lithely into the back of the small vehicle.

During the drive Samantha kept up a flow of conversation with Luke which totally and deliberately excluded Gemma, and from which she discerned that Samantha was a very important part of the social life of the island and that she and her uncle lived in an extremely luxurious villa just outside the main town of Georgetown.

To Gemma's surprise, after driving through the capital Luke carried on to Samantha's home.

There was a very pregnant silence as he stopped the buggy in the drive, and Gemma was once again conscious of Samantha's dislike as the other girl got out, and coaxed Luke pleadingly, 'Do stay and eat with us, darling, I'm sure your friend won't mind.'

Her stare challenged Gemma to dare to object but, before she could say a word, Luke was saying smoothly. 'Gemma might not, but I would, I'm afraid. I'm just not up to a game of chess with your uncle tonight. Give him my regards, though, and tell him I'll be in touch soon.'

He had put the buggy in gear before Samantha could object, and within seconds they were speeding back down on to the tarmac road.

'Sorry about that,' Luke apologised when they were once again through the town.

'There's nothing to apologise for,' Gemma managed lightly. 'It's only natural that your ... your girlfriend should want your company, especially as you've been away.'

She saw his eyebrow lift sardonically at her use of the word 'girlfriend', but he made no comment, apart from saying coolly, 'Samantha likes to play-act. At the moment she's enjoying imagining she's in love with me. It won't last.'

It was plain to Gemma that however real or imagined the other girl's feelings might be, Luke did not reciprocate them—further confirmation, had she needed it, of the control he exercised over his emotional life, and his aversion to any sort of real commitment.

They had now turned off the tarmac road and were driving along a bumpy track and through what was obviously a building site. A row of Portacabins ran alongside the track with gaps here and there where materials had been delivered. To Gemma's left lay the sea, sparkling beneath the silver glitter of the moon, and she caught her breath at the beauty of it. The road ran alongside the beach, silver white in the moonlight and studded with clumps of palms. She had to blink several times before she could accept that it was real.

'Are you glad now that you didn't turn tail at the airport and run?' Luke asked her mockingly, shocking her with the accuracy with which he had read her emotions and thoughts. Instead of replying to him she compressed her mouth and looked the other way.

Right at the outset, Luke had told Gemma that he would provide the accommodation, and until now it had not occurred to her to query this. Now as she looked around at the deserted beach and shadowy clumps of Portacabins, she wondered where on earth she was going to live. If anything, she had envisaged staying at perhaps a small hotel, or a villa, but now she began to wonder if Luke meant to house her in one of these cabins. What she had seen of the back streets of Georgetown as they drove through, and on the drive from the airport, had not reassured her as to the quality of the local habitation, but suddenly the road swerved; the beach started to shelve away and behind them rose cliffs.

The long, shadowed finger of a jetty stretched out into the sea and two or three small speedboats bobbed at their moorings alongside it. Beyond the jetty, and beyond the reef itself, lay the long shape of an expensive ocean-going yacht. It was well illuminated, and Gemma gazed at it in awe, admiring its sleek lines.

'Like it?' Luke asked her in an offhand fashion, bringing the buggy to a halt alongside the jetty.

'Mm, she's beautiful. Who does she belong to?'

'Me,' Luke told her laconically. 'Come on.' He opened the buggy door for her, having lithely leapt over his and come round to her side. 'Don't worry about the luggage, one of the men will ferry it out. You look ready to fall asleep on your feet. For the moment we can't bring the *Minerva* in close enough to moor her to the jetty—we'll need to deepen the harbour before we can do that—but these little speedboats are easy enough to handle; you'll soon get the hang of it. Come on.'

In a bemused daze, Gemma allowed Luke to bustle her on to the jetty and down into the first of the bobbing boats. The yacht belonged to Luke. She could hardly take it in.

'Do you mean . . .' She swallowed and started again. 'Did you mean that I'd be living on the yacht?'

'Yes, any objections? We won't be alone, if that's what's bugging you,' he added sardonically. 'She holds a full complement of staff, and crew.'

Gemma was glad that she was sitting with her face in the shadows so that Luke couldn't see the embarrassed burn of colour that scorched her skin.

'I'm not totally naïve, Luke,' she managed to retort. 'You're hardly likely to have designs on me while there are women like Samantha about.'

'You think not? Don't be too sure.'

He was just being gallant, she told herself, just flirting automatically with her, and it didn't mean a thing, but even so she could feel the blood beating through her veins, accompanied by a curious sense of weightlessness which she tried to ascribe to exhaustion.

One of the members of Luke's crew helped them on board, and while Luke excused himself to catch up on his outstanding messages, Gemma was shown to what were to be her quarters for the duration of her stay.

Their magnificence left her completely lost for words. In addition to a bedroom which possessed an enormous king-size bed, she had a bathroom, and a dressing-room lined with wardrobes and mirrors, plus her own private sitting-room equipped with telephone, desk, settee, television, and even a small dining-table and two chairs.

She was so quiet that the steward asked her anxiously, 'Is it not to your liking?'

Not to her liking! Gemma swallowed hard. Her small Manchester flatlet would have fitted into the bedroom and still left space over.

'It . . . it's fabulous,' she managed at last and was

rewarded with a beaming smile.

'It is the guest suite, and Mr Luke he told us to have it specially prepared for you. If you want something to eat, the chef he suggests perhaps a salad and some of our king-sized prawns.'

She hadn't thought she was hungry, but suddenly the thought of food was tempting. It was too early to go to bed yet, and if she did, she would be awake in the early hours, suffering the effects of jet lag.

While she waited for the steward to return with her supper, and for her luggage to arrive, Gemma wandered around her suite, gazing at everything with awe.

The mahogany furniture and panels in the sitting-room gleamed richly in the soft light from the Christopher Wray lamps. The settee was upholstered in an exclusive British chintz, and the carpet had quite obviously been woven especially to pick out the soft blue in the pretty pink, blue and green colourway of the creamy background fabric.

Bookshelves packed with leather-bound volumes flanked a fake fireplace; the desk provided for her use was a beautiful Regency antique, and carefully arranged in front on top of the desk was a selection of stationery bearing the name of the yacht. Gemma touched the thick paper with tense fingers. How her mother would have loved this! A piece of Meissen china was artfully arranged on the sofa table behind the settee, and a bowl of fresh flowers decorated the coffee table, which also held the very latest glossy magazines.

She wandered into her bedroom, touching the thick quilted cotton bedspread. This room echoed the same soft colours as her sitting-room. She stroked the pillowcases. Percale cotton. No expense had been spared.

There were even matching towels in the bathroom, with its marble sanitary wear and brass fittings. A huge mirror on one wall enhanced the small space and green plants massed in one corner gave the room an air of tropical splendour.

A discreet rap at her outer door made her walk bemusedly back into her sitting-room. The same steward who had shown her to her suite was back, carrying a tray with her supper. The salad had been arranged with exquisite artistry, the prawns so succulent-looking and fresh that she could feel her mouth watering.

A china tea service in a design she recognised as Spode was deposited on her round dining-table, a chair solicitously pulled out so that she could sit down. Not until he had assured himself that she was served with everything that she might need did her steward retire.

It was like stepping into a fantasy, Gemma thought dreamily as she finished her meal. She felt as though she had to keep reaching out to touch things to reassure herself that it was all real.

CHAPTER SEVEN

GEMMA'S first day in her new employment did not begin well. For a start, despite all her good intentions, she overslept, waking only when a steward came in with a tray of tea.

'Mr O'Rourke said to tell you that if you sleep any longer it will only make the jet lag worse,' he informed Gemma, grinning at her when she realised what time it was.

Ten o'clock in the morning! What on earth must Luke think of her?

She rushed through her tea and showered and dressed at speed. The steward had told her that Luke was in his own private office, and had given her instructions as to how to find it.

It was exactly ten forty-five when she knocked on the imposing polished door.

Luke opened it himself, his eyebrows lifting in patent surprise when he saw her standing there.

'I'm sorry I overslept,' she began to apologise, but he cut her off with a negative wave of his hand, frowning at her thoughtfully as he studied her pale face and worried eyes.

'You can't possibly have had time to have breakfast. My message to the steward wasn't designed to have the effect on you that it evidently did. You mustn't try to rush about here too much until you're properly acclimatised, Gemma, and that will take several days.'

Several days! But he had brought her here to work, not to laze around like a holidaymaker.

When she said as much he laughed. 'Oh, you won't be wasting time. I'm going to give you the men's files to read so that you can familiarise yourself with their names and occupations, and then, perhaps tomorrow, I'll take you round the site. Today, though, you will rest and find your feet, and the first thing you're going to do is to have a proper breakfast.'

It must be the change of climate that was making her so biddable, Gemma decided ten minutes later as another white-jacketed steward held out her seat for her in the private dining area in Luke's quarters.

The dining area had sliding glass doors that were open to the tropical heat, and it overlooked the yacht's pool and deck space.

The freshly squeezed tropical fruit juice and muesli cereal placed in front of her were too tempting for Gemma to resist, although she did refuse the offer of scrambled eggs and toast.

'Heavens, if I eat like this all the time I'm here, I'll grow enormous,' she complained to Luke, as she accepted a second cup of coffee.

'Make the most if it,' he teased her warningly. 'You'll be working so hard later on that you'll need your energy.'

From the deck of the yacht she could see the construction site, and hear the sounds of the heavy plant being used there. While they drank their coffee Luke produced a plan of what the complex would look like once it was completed, and the ambitious scope of it almost took Gemma's breath away. It truly would be a holidaymakers' paradise, once it was finished.

'This afternoon I'll show you the other side of the island—not the glamour of the hotels, but the reality of what life can be like here for some of the people.'

Poverty and deprivation would always touch him like this, Gemma suspected, because he had once known them for himself. How many other men would channel those memories to positive actions on behalf of others? So many self-made men preferred to lock away their youthful memories of poverty and hardship as though in some way they were detrimental to them. Or was it that they were so haunted by them that to release them from their deepest memories would somehow act as a bad luck charm on their success? She was venturing into emotional territory about which she knew very little, Gemma realised, acknowledging that it would be pointless for her to pursue such an avenue of thought.

'We'll wait until it gets a little cooler; because of the yacht's air conditioning you'll probably find it takes you a little longer to get acclimatised.'

Gemma nibbled on her bottom lip as she tried to think of the best way to bring up something that was bothering her.

'Is something wrong?' Luke questioned, accurately reading her mind.

'Well, yes, and no ... Luke, I feel very guilty about staying here in all this luxury. Your other employees...'

'Are all male, and none of them are also personal friends. St George's might look a very relaxed and carefree place, but it isn't always as safe as it looks. You have to bear in mind that quite a considerable proportion of the population lives in conditions of appalling poverty.

'Petty thieving, often with violence, can be quite

common. That's why most of the hotels advise their
guests to stay within the confines of their grounds, or,
when they do go outside, not to wear expensive
jewellery, or to carry cameras or large sums of money.
The men who are working for me here, and who have
come from Britain, in the main share rented accommodation—I can hardly see your parents being pleased at
the thought of you shacking up with half a dozen
unattached males, can you? Nor would I myself feel
happy about the idea of you living alone, and the nearest
hotel is several miles away down the coast, which would
mean that I would have to provide you with transport
and possibly a driver as well. So all in all I decided it
would be best if you stayed here on board the *Minerva*.
Any objections?'

What female in her right mind could object to such
luxurious surroundings? Samantha for instance would
probably leap at the chance. So why did she feel so
uncomfortable with the situation? Was it because she
feared that the men might not take her seriously once
they knew she and Luke were personal friends? Surely it
wasn't Luke himself she feared? No ... no, it wasn't
that, even though his sexuality did cause more than the
odd *frisson* of response to run through her body from
time to time.

Instead of doing all this mental agonising she should
be grateful that Luke had taken such pains over her
comfort and accommodation, Gemma chided herself.
Just this brief foray on to the deck to look across the
lagoon at the construction site had brought home to her
how enervating the climate could be. Her thin cotton
shirt was already soaked through with perspiration, her
skin prickling with heat and discomfort.

'Perhaps if I took some of those files and studied them sitting out here on the deck, I might be able to start getting acclimatised,' she suggested.

'Good idea, but don't overdo it, and remember to sit in the shade, and to keep yourself covered up; we don't want you going down with either heat or sun stroke. Come with me and I'll show you where the files are kept.'

They were back in his study, and as he motioned her forwards to show her how the lock on the cabinet worked Gemma found herself having to squeeze past him. Awareness of him as a man flooded hotly through her body, making her tremble and tense, all too conscious of the heat and weight of his arm against her body as he drew her forwards to look at the cabinet.

He felt her tremble and frowned down at her, unexpectedly placing one cool hand against her throat and making her pulse jump in frantic excitement.

'Do you feel feverish? You're looking very pale.'

'No . . . no, it must just have been the shock of the air conditioning after the heat outside,' she fibbed to explain away her shivery reaction to his touch. 'I'm fine, Luke, don't fuss. You're beginning to make me feel like a fragile Victorian female,' she teased him, trying to shake off her disturbing awareness of him.

'Maybe that's because I think you are—fragile, not Victorian. Girls like you with wealthy parents are always fragile, because you've never been exposed to the realities of life.'

'I teach at a North Mancester comprehensive school, Luke,' Gemma reminded him, suddenly angered by his assumptions about her. 'I'm not fragile at all.'

'Yes you are. You always have been. You've been

protected all your life, like a rare piece of glass swaddled in cotton wool, far too delicate to be touched by rough uncouth hands,' he told her broodingly.

Gemma couldn't understand what had got into him, but he was wrong about her. Her parents might have tried to preserve around her the rarified atmosphere Luke was describing, but she had never allowed them to do so.

'If you think I'm so helpless and delicate, I'm surprised you wanted me out here,' she snapped, suddenly almost resenting him.

The phone on his desk rang, abruptly shattering the tension. Luke opened the drawer and thrust a pile of files into her hands before striding over to pick up the receiver.

Standing at such close confines to him, Gemma could hardly avoid hearing Samantha's voice.

It became apparent that the other girl was inviting him out for lunch, but Luke refused.

Samantha's voice grew querulous and then bitter as Luke resisted her arguments, and, feeling acutely *de trop*, Gemma moved towards the door. She had almost reached it when Luke's hand shot out and pinioned her wrist. Without looking at her, he said into the receiver, 'Samantha, this has gone far enough. As I told you before I left for London, what we had between us was good as far as it went, but now it's over. Now be a good girl, and go and find someone else to play with.'

Gemma felt the heat scorch her own skin at the stinging contempt in the last few words. She wanted to berate him for it on behalf of her sex, and also to berate him for his lack of discretion in speaking like that to Samantha while she was in earshot.

As he replaced the receiver he released her, studying her flushed face and angry eyes with cool composure.

'Don't look like that. All your sex aren't like you, you know. Some of them can be pretty thick-skinned when it suits them. Samantha knew the score right from the start, and if she chooses to change the rules now, then she must accept the fact that I don't want to abide by those changes.'

'Your ... your relationship with her is scarcely any concern of mine,' Gemma told him huskily, unable to stop herself from adding, 'Luke, you were so unkind to her. If she loves you ...'

'Loves me!' He laughed acidly. 'Oh, my God, you're even more naïve than I thought. Samantha loves no one other than herself. It's a game to her, Gemma, and I'm just one in a long line of players. Because this time I was the one who called the shots she doesn't want the game to end. I know what you're thinking; that it's ungentlemanly of me to tell you all this, but I have my reasons. I don't want you getting the wrong idea about my relationship with Samantha.'

'Oh, I think it's quite obvious what your relationship is.'

'Was,' Luke corrected her tersely. 'In the past tense, Gemma. It's over.'

'Luke, it's really no concern of mine.'

'So cool,' he mocked, cutting her off. 'How ladylike, Gemma. Your mother would be proud of you.'

'I'd better go and study these files.' She was backing down and she knew it, but suddenly the atmosphere inside the study was too intense, too charged with the magnetic aura of Luke's sexuality, and she was retreating from it like the nervous virgin that she was.

He let her go, but she was still shaking when she got up on deck. A steward materialised at her side as though by magic, and produced a table and chair for her, carefully placed to shade her from the strong sun.

She had been working for almost an hour when Luke's shadow fell across the bar of sunlight just beyond her shadowed corner, and she looked up at him warily.

'I came to remind you not to stay out here for much longer. We'll be having lunch soon. Some of the management team from the site will be joining us so that I can introduce you to them, and tonight we've been invited to dine at Government House. You'll find it very interesting. The Governor's wife is very interested in education, it's one of her pet hobby horses, and she'll be able to give you a lot of help and advice about how to deal with the people here.'

So tonight's dinner was business rather than pleasure, and she as Luke's employee wasn't allowed to refuse to go.

Lunch was a pleasantly informal meal. Gemma was seated between the captain and Luke. Luke had introduced her to Captain Ericson beforehand, and she had found the tall, fair-headed Swede to be extremely knowledgeable about the Caribbean.

He was somewhere in his forties, Gemma judged, and it was apparent from his conversation that he had served in the navy for many years and also that Luke's yacht was not the first luxury vessel he had commanded.

Gemma could see that there was both liking and respect between the two men, and Luke left it to Captain Ericson to answer her questions about the yacht, explaining that he was its second owner, and that before committing himself to acquiring it he had sought the advice of Captain Ericson, who had sailed in her under the previous owner.

Gemma couldn't help comparing Luke's attitude to those of some of her parents' friends. She sensed that Luke wasn't particularly possession-orientated and he admitted quite readily that he would never have thought of buying the yacht if he hadn't needed a base from which to oversee the Caribbean venture.

'So what will happen to her when the complex is completed?' she asked him.

'Oh, I shall keep her, I think, maybe even lease her out; I don't know yet.'

The arrival of the other men had brought their discussion about the *Minerva* to a halt, and Gemma soon discovered that Luke's management team wasn't anything like as relaxed with her as Captain Ericson had been.

She had always been sensitive to the feelings of others and she knew straight away that the men felt uneasy in her company.

Was it because she was a woman? She assumed it must be.

'This is Ian Cameron, my chief engineer,' Luke told her, introducing a burly, sandy-haired Scot to her, 'and Tom Maiden, who's in charge of making sure our raw materials arrive when and where we want them—a sort of glorified quantity surveyor.'

Tom Maiden was somewhere near her father's age, and he smiled cautiously at her.

The other two men were in charge of personnel and building operations respectively, and Gemma sensed that Harry Barker, the personnel manager, in particular was reserving judgement on her.

'All of you know why Gemma is out here, of course.'

Was it her imagination or had she really seen that expressive look that passed between Ian Cameron and Harry Barker? And if she hadn't imagined it, what had it meant?

Gemma was still worrying about that look when they reached the coffee stage of the meal.

All the men had listened politely to her contribution to the conversation, and, from what they had said, none of them had come across as being anti career women, which in itself was something of a surprise, knowing the macho image of the building industry. So why was she getting such strong vibrations of doubt and even distrust from them?

Did they think she wasn't up to the job? Did they mistrust her friendship with Luke and fear that she could spy on them on his behalf? This last idea seemed ridiculous when she listened to the way the five men joked with one another. It was obvious that Luke had their respect and their loyalty, and, although he permitted a certain amount of gentle ribbing, Gemma had little doubt that he was able to make sure his commands were obeyed immediately whenever necessary.

'Gemma's been going through the men's files,' she heard Luke saying. 'And tonight, I'm taking her to Government House to meet the Governor's wife, who as you all know is very keen on establishing a better form of adult education for the people on the island.'

'Have you anything in mind yet?' Harry Barker questioned Gemma when Luke had finished.

'Nothing definite, just a few ideas that I'll need to toss around with you. Luke has told me that the sort of qualifications and education the men want will be something equivalent to our HNCs, and I was hoping it might be possible to split the men up into various groups—those who want to study as electricians, those who want to concentrate on heating and plumbing, and so on, for a variety of trades, but I'd welcome your views on the subject.'

Harry Barker's expression had changed from doubt to grudging approval and now he nodded his head, and said gruffly, 'Well, you're certainly thinking along the right lines. A good basic grounding in a variety of trades is exactly what's needed, and that way we'll be able to employ some of them on the maintenance and permanent staff once the complex is finished.'

'Yes, Luke was telling me that, apart from the holiday industry, there are very few employment opportunities on the island.'

Although she could see that the men were unbending a little towards her, there was still an unbridgeable distance, and when they all stood up to leave, she couldn't help noticing the covert looks they gave, first to her and then to Luke.

Half an hour after lunch, Luke also disappeared in the direction of the complex, giving her a promise that he would return later to give her a tour of the island's less salubrious areas before they got ready for dinner.

In the two hours she had to wait for him, Gemma read some more files. She was appalled to discover how early teenagers left school and how few and far between the opportunities for higher education were. As she pondered the problem, she had a mental vision of her own late pupils the last time she had seen them; in the present climate of high unemployment, were *they* really any better off? Standards of education might be higher; but, as she herself had seen, with the prospect of no job ahead of them when they left school many young people were simply not bothering to learn.

What was the point, they had demanded of her during an end-of-term discussion just before she left, when the qualifications they were likely to get would do nothing to help them get work? She had been lost for an answer then and still was now. Would she herself have worked so hard at school if she had not had the lure of independence in front of her?

Here at least she would be teaching young adults, people with hope in their hearts and at least a reasonable chance of putting their skills to work. The cynically old and knowing faces of her ex-pupils haunted her at times. In her heart of hearts she felt as guilty as though she had deliberately abandoned them. She had been told during her training that she was really too sensitive to make a good teacher, and she was beginning to wonder if that was perhaps true.

When the heat of the afternoon finally drove her into her suite, she showered, and then wrapped herself in a loose cotton robe and went to lie down on her bed.

The air conditioning was bliss after the heat outside. She was very tired. It wouldn't hurt to close her eyes for a few minutes ...

It was the rattle of the tea things that woke her. She opened her eyes, wondering for a moment where she was.

'Gemma? Are you awake?'

There was a brief rap on the door and then Luke walked in. She was sitting up, unaware of how closely the fine cotton clung to her sleep-warmed skin until she saw the way Luke's attention narrowed on her body.

When she did glance down, she flushed deep scarlet when she realised how sheer the fine cotton actually was. The dusky rose of her nipples was quite clearly visible. She moved hurriedly, turning her back on him, her voice muffled as she explained that she had just woken up.

'There's no need for the shy, maidenly act, Gemma.' His voice seemed to grate harshly over the cool air. 'I'm hardly naïve enough to believe I'm the first man to see you wearing so little.'

He was judging her by his own standards, Gemma realised, and he was far too worldly and experienced to suspect that he was wrong. He *was* the first and the only man, but she certainly wasn't going to tell him so.

'I wasn't acting,' she said stiffly in self-defence. 'I'm just not used to my employer wandering into my bedroom.'

It was a slight exaggeration of the facts, but she felt that she had made her point until he replied smoothly, 'Employee and employer, is that how you see us?'

'Aren't those our roles?' Gemma countered, suppressing a sudden *frisson* of disquiet.

He smiled mockingly at her. 'One of them, certainly, but there have been others, haven't there? Pupil and teacher for instance, and even teacher and pupil ...'

Gemma couldn't pretend not to know what he meant and she felt her skin flush scarlet at his reference to that long ago lesson in kissing she had begged him to give her. Was he never going to let that drop?

'Tell me, Gemma,' he asked smoothly now, 'did he appreciate your expertise?'

In a stiff voice she complained huskily, 'Luke, what

are you trying to do? I was fourteen and I . . .'

'Didn't know any better? Didn't know that nice well brought-up girls don't ask road gang navvies to kiss them? You're lying, Gemma; you knew all right.'

She couldn't deny it, but still she burst out impassionately, 'You were my friend and that was how I turned to you—as my friend. Can't we forget it now, Luke? I . . .'

Appallingly she felt tears sting her eyes, and quickly averted her head, but, as though he had seen them, Luke's voice changed abruptly. 'I'm sorry. You'll have to put my bad behaviour down to a mixture of jet lag and heat. What I really came down here for was to bring you some tea and to see if you still wanted to go for that drive.'

'Do you?' she asked doubtfully. 'Or are you too tired, if you're suffering from jet lag?'

'I don't like sleeping during the day. At least, not unless there's someone sleeping beside me,' he told her outrageously. 'Get dressed,' he added, 'and then I'll take you out.' He glanced at the wristwatch he was wearing. 'We've got a couple of hours before we need to get ready for dinner.'

Remembering her ride in the buggy the previous evening, Gemma dressed in a cotton shirt and matching jeans, and she couldn't help feeling pleased by the approving look Luke gave her when she joined him in her sitting-room.

'Sensible girl,' he praised. 'I meant to warn you not to wear anything too provocative. Both sexes here like, as they say in common parlance, to "look with their hands"—a rather disconcerting experience if you're not used to it. And since their own moral code permits both men and women to have as many lovers as they wish, before marriage, they don't understand that, when they see a European woman scantily dressed, it doesn't necessarily mean that she's sexually available.'

There was a spectacular tropical shower of rain just before they set out, a downpour that lasted for approximately fifteen minutes before ceasing as abruptly as it had started, but by the time they had gone ashore and driven into Georgetown the streets were already drying in the hot sun.

It was the back-street areas not normally seen by tourists that Luke showed her: a veritable shanty town of wooden shacks, so small and often haphazardly constructed that Gemma couldn't believe they were actually people's homes.

When she commented on them, Luke pointed out fairly, 'You have to remember that this isn't Europe and that the people spend far more time out of doors, but I agree with all that you're saying, nonetheless.'

They toured the mean, claustrophobic streets for some time, Gemma shivering occasionally as she saw the gangs of black youths sullenly watching their progress. Again Luke reminded her that they could scarcely be blamed for their resentment.

'Most of them, if they have jobs, are paid a pittance for working in hotels where they are in daily contact with Europeans who in their eyes possess untold riches. And St George's is far from being the worst island in this respect—far from it. It's one of the more wealthy islands.'

Gemma was very subdued and thoughtful when they went back on board the *Minerva*. The last thing she felt like doing was going out for dinner, but she was after all in Luke's employ, not his guest, and so she went through the clothes that one of the stewards had unpacked and put away, looking for something suitable to wear.

Since they were dining at Government House, she suspected the other guests would be extremely sophisticated and that she would need to dress accordingly.

Luckily she had something suitable with her, a silk dress she had packed on some unnamed impulse, and which, although simple, had been extremely expensive, and showed it.

It didn't take her long to shower and do her hair. She kept her make-up to a minimum, surprised to discover that she had already caught the sun even though she had rigorously kept to the shade.

When she mentioned this to Luke later he reminded her that he had warned her that in the tropics a fair European skin could burn even in the shade, and even through a fine cotton shirt.

Luckily she wasn't sore, but she made a mental note to make sure that she was well protected by suntan cream whenever she went out to the site. She was lucky in the fact that because of her slightly olive skin tone she tanned easily and well. She dreaded to think what it must be like out here for the truly fair-skinned. No wonder that it was on those islands that backed on to the Atlantic sea that the first Europeans had built their homes, so that they caught the invigorating winds coming off that ocean.

She knew that she had chosen the right dress when she saw that Luke was wearing a white dinner jacket. He looked so at home and at ease in his evening clothes that even she found it impossible to remember the gangly boy who had been so awkward of the social niceties.

As though he, too, shared her thoughts, he gave her a wry smile and said softly, 'Fine feathers, Gemma: don't let them deceive you. I'm still the same Luke underneath.'

Funnily, though, he said it not as a reassurance but as a warning; but a warning against what, Gemma wondered, as she allowed him to help her down into the waiting launch that was to take them to the shore.

The Jeep Luke used to drive them to Government House had a canvas roof which protected Gemma's hair from the breeze, and he had timed their arrival well, as they were neither the first nor the last.

A little to her surprise, Gemma discovered that she took to the Governor's wife straight away, and Luke left her talking together while he went off to renew acquaintances with some of the other guests.

'You wouldn't believe how many of my friends with unmarried daughters have been pressing me to invite them out here since I made the mistake of telling them that Luke was a regular visitor,' she told Gemma. 'Of course, I've tried to tell them that they're wasting their time and that he isn't the marrying kind—and if he was, I can't see him picking a pretty little débutante, with nothing between her ears but fluff, can you?'

'Not really.' Gemma smiled, too.

'You've known him a long time, I gather.' She gave Gemma a distinctly speculative look.

When had Luke told the Governor's wife that? 'Since I was a teenager,' Gemma told her calmly.

'Mmm . . . Well of course there's bound to be a certain amount of gossip, especially since you're living on board his yacht, but you can rely on me to do what I can to quench it. I'm surprised that Samantha isn't here tonight. Have you met her yet?'

'Yes, she picked us up from the airport,' Gemma responded. It was a shock to learn that people would gossip about her and Luke, and as though she guessed what she was thinking the Govenor's wife said gently, 'I'm sorry, I didn't mean to upset you, but this is a very small and very parochial island, and when we have a man like Luke living among us, we can't help being interested in what's going on.

'A word of warning to you, though, my dear, if I may. Samantha can be a very vindictive young woman when she's thwarted. Unfortunately, because of her uncle, she does have a certain standing on this island.'

Gemma frowned. What was the Governor's wife trying to tell her? Samantha was Luke's affair and not hers.

'I'm afraid she's bruiting it all over the place that Luke brought you here not so much to work with him, as to . . . well, quite frankly, my dear—to warm his bed.'

Gemma was shocked and it showed. She put down the glass of wine she was holding with shaking fingers.

What on earth had possessed Samantha to spread such vicious lies? Suddenly she wondered uneasily if that was why the men had reacted so oddly to her at lunchtime. Had they already heard these rumours of Samantha's? It seemed unlikely, but then, as the Governor's wife had just reminded her, St George's was a very small island, and in certain circles everyone did know everyone else.

'My dear, I'm so sorry,' the Governor's wife apologised contritely, touching her wrist lightly. 'I didn't mean to upset you. I hadn't realised it would come as such a shock to you.'

Perhaps she was being naïve not to have guessed what

interpretation people would put on the fact that she was living on board Luke's yacht.

'Luke and I ... we're friends ... that's all.'

Inside she was a mass of seething confusion and distress. She would have to talk to Luke about this at the first opportunity, but not here. She would have to contain herself somehow until they were back on board the *Minerva*. Somehow for the rest of the evening she would have to try and behave as though she was completely unaware of the speculation and curiosity seething around them. Now, as though veils had been ripped from her eyes, she could see how covertly people *were* watching her. How dared Samantha do this to her? she wondered sickly. That other women could be so venomous shocked her. She had never been exposed to this type of female vindictiveness before and, now that she was, she had no idea how to cope with it.

'Are you sure you're all right, or would you like me to find Luke?' The Governor's wife was looking round vaguely, and Gemma clutched wildly at her.

The very last person she wanted to face right now was Luke. 'No ... please, I'm fine now.' She managed a rather pallid smile.

'Well, if you're sure.' Her hostess sounded so doubtful that Gemma was forced to reassure her that she was quite recovered. Luckily another guest came up to claim her attention, leaving Gemma free to slip away to the room set aside as a ladies' cloakroom, which fortunately was empty.

She stayed there as long as she dared, forcing herself to ignore the panic and pain hurtling round her body. In any other circumstances the gossip would have been laughable. What on earth would Luke want with a woman like her? If she had simply been his guest she could have afforded to outface Samantha's vicious gossip, but she wasn't his guest, she was his employee, and how could she gain the respect and trust of her co-workers, when they suspected that she and Luke were lovers?

It was an impossible and intolerable situation, but since she couldn't discuss it with Luke here in public she would just have to pretend that everything was normal.

How many pairs of eyes would be studying her and Luke tonight, waiting for some sign that Samantha's lies were true? she wondered despairingly as she went reluctantly back to join the other guests.

CHAPTER EIGHT

'YOU were very quiet tonight. Are you feeling all right?'

As he had done once before, Luke placed his cool hand against her throat, measuring the frantic race of her pulse, but this time she jumped back, her body as rigid as stone.

'Gemma.' He was frowning. 'What on earth . . .'

'Luke, I need to talk to you.'

They were standing up on deck, in both sight and sound of any of the crew who might happen to walk past. 'But not here. Could we . . . could we go to my sitting-room?'

She *had* to tell him about the gossip. He would be as disturbed by it as she was herself. But what could he do to squash it, apart from sending her home?

And then she knew the reason behind all the turmoil that had torn her apart this evening. She didn't want to go home. She didn't want to leave him.

There was scarcely time for the enormity of this realisation to sink in before he was taking her arm, and saying softly, 'Of course, come on.'

He waited until they were safely inside her sitting-room before speaking again.

'Now, Gemma, what's the matter?'

There was no easy way to tell him, and feeling extremely uncomfortable she blurted out, 'The Governor's wife told me tonight that people are gossiping

137

about us . . . that . . . that someone . . . that someone has started a rumour that you didn't bring me here to work for you so much as to . . .'

'Share my bed?' Luke finished softly for her.

Her eyes widened slightly, registering her own inner shock; not because he had anticipated her, but because of the expression on his face. It was at once both derisive and challenging.

'And is sharing my bed such a difficult thing for you to envisage, Gemma. Why? Because of Hardman or because of what I am?

'There are some pretty little rich girls who find it quite a turn on to have sex with their social inferiors . . . "rough trade" our transatlantic cousins call it.' His mouth twisted in taunting mockery as he studied her pale shocked face. 'But obviously you aren't one of them.'

'Unlike Samantha,' Gemma suggested acidly, suddenly coming out of her stunned paralysis to fight back against the bitterness of his taunts.

He had changed so quickly from the Luke she thought she knew, to this dangerous, mocking stranger, that she could hardly believe it. And to accuse her of all people of thinking him beneath her! Surely he knew her better than that.

Immediately she mentioned Samantha's name his eyes narrowed. 'Like Samantha,' he agreed softly. 'Was she the one who started the rumour, Gemma?'

Her refusal to answer gave her away.

'Well, well, she's got more intelligence than I gave her credit for.'

It took several minutes for his meaning to percolate

through to her brain, and even then it was only because of the almost insolently sexual way he was studying her body that she realised what he meant.

All at once her stomach muscles clenched, the breath leaking from her lungs on a thready gasp of shock. Luke wanted her. She opened her mouth and then closed it again, shaking her head in bewildered disbelief as her eyes darkened with pain.

'Luke, you didn't give me this job just to . . ,?'

'Just to manoeuvre you into my bed?' he taunted. 'Not entirely, but I won't deny that, shall we say, it was one of the deciding factors.'

'But . . .'

'But what? But a man with my background shouldn't even dare to aspire to such giddy heights; is that what you're trying to tell me, Gemma? That I'm not good enough to go to bed with? But I was good enough to ask for lessons in loving, wasn't I? Did Hardman appreciate what I taught you?' he asked, savagely changing tack.

'Luke, please . . .'

'Please what?' he laughed goadingly.

'Luke, you don't mean this. You don't want me. You wouldn't even like . . .'

'What I'd like, lady, is to roll you on to your back and make love to you until the only sounds coming from that soft mouth of yours are moans of pleasure.'

The shock of his words reverberated through her entire body, until it seemed to Gemma that no part of her remained untouched by the raw sexuality of them. Instinctively she knew that he wasn't lying and that he did want her, and dangerously her own senses caught fire from his, and without the slightest effort at all, she could oh so easily imagine him making love to her, making her body and her heart sing with pleasure.

Panic burst through the daze of sudden excitement gripping her, reminding her of how impossible it was for her and Luke to become lovers. She was already too emotionally involved with him; if she allowed him to become her lover . . . She shivered suddenly, remembering that Luke wasn't a man who wanted any kind of permanent commitment, and she certainly wasn't a woman who could ever enjoy the type of ephemeral affairs that he indulged in.

No, it was better to stop this thing right now. It would hurt to leave, but how much greater the hurt would be if she stayed.

Gathering her courage, she took a deep breath and stepped forward. 'I think it would be best if I left, Luke. I'll get myself a seat on the first flight out of the island, and in the meantime I think I ought to book myself a room at a hotel.' She forced herself to look directly at him, and almost flinched as she saw the savage mockery in his eyes.

'Nice try, but it won't work. You're under contract to me, Gemma, and if you break it . . .'

'My contract says nothing about going to bed with you.'

His mouth tightened and he said harshly, 'For God's sake, Gemma, you can scarcely think that I mean to force you into bed with me.' He paused for a moment to let his words sink in. 'I've never had to force a woman to have sex with me, and I'm not about to start now. If I put my mind to it, I suspect I could quite easily overcome both your scruples and your distaste for my inferior social status, but I won't.'

'Luke, for heaven's sake, I don't think of you as a social inferior. Surely you must know that? You're putting me in the same mould as my parents and their friends, and I thought you knew that I don't judge people by their position in life or their wealth. I never have.'

'But you still won't go to bed with me,' he taunted, watching her.

Gemma bit her lip, wondering what she could say. If she admitted to him that she was already frightened by the depths of her emotional and physical response to him, in his present mood he might just decide to take advantage of her vulnerability.

'I wouldn't go to bed with any man that I didn't love, no matter what his social and financial standing. That's not the way I live my life.'

Suddenly his expression changed, lightened, and the smile he gave her was the one she was familiar with.

'I'm sorry, Gemma. You're right of course.' He turned his back to her and said quietly, 'If you do decide to go home I'll arrange everything for you, but the fact that I desire you was only one of the reasons I brought you out here. There's still a job for you to do.

A job she wanted to do, Gemma acknowledged, but how could she when she knew that people were gossiping about them? But gossip could only hurt when it was true. She would prove to everyone that she could do the job ... She would prove that ...

That what? That she wasn't in the least attracted to Luke? But she was. She had known that this evening before they had quarrelled. Knowing that physically he wanted her made her acutely aware of the fact that she desired him, too. She had known it at home when he had kissed her, but she had deliberately suppressed that knowledge. Now she could suppress it no longer. And what made it worse was that, no matter how foolish she was being, she knew that she was going to stay on the island.

She took a deep breath and said huskily, 'I'm staying.'

'Good girl.' There was admiration as well as desire in the look he gave her, and Gemma knew that if he touched her now . . . if he took her in his arms and kissed her . . . But he wasn't touching her; he was moving away from her, and when she made an instinctive movement towards him he shook his head.

'My control is finite, Gemma. Nothing's changed. I still want you. I've wanted you since that day by the river,' he added almost broodingly, anger flaring bitterly in his eyes for a second as he added, 'That was a hell of a thing to do to a man, you know, to ask him to teach you how to make love to someone else. And there was so much more than how to kiss that I wanted to teach you. I wanted to teach you the pleasure that comes from a man's hands and lips caressing your breasts, I wanted to teach you how . . .'

'Stop it. Stop it, Luke.' She was shivering under the onslaught of the *frissons* of arousal running through her nerve endings, aching for him to follow his words with their actions, and yet knowing that to encourage him to do so would be the utmost folly.

'But someone else taught you those things . . . taught you how to appreciate the pleasure of being a woman.'

Someone else . . . Gemma's heart caught in her throat

as she realised that he didn't know the truth.

He walked over to the door and opened it. 'Oh, and you needn't worry that I'll go back on my word and make a grab for you. You know that I want you, Gemma. If you ever change your mind it will be up to you to come to me. Is that understood?'

Ridiculously she found herself nodding her head. What was she doing? Of course she wasn't going to change her mind, and if she had any sense at all she would be on the first flight home. But she didn't want to go home. She wanted . . . She wanted the impossible, she acknowledged miserably, as the full force of her real feelings hit her. She wanted Luke's love!

She couldn't sleep, and after trying to for over an hour, she got up and pulled on her clothes, making her way up on to the deck.

One of the hands nodded respectfully at her as she walked past him. Of course, the crew must work shifts; someone had to look after the yacht and their safety during the night. Even at night the air was still warm, and she went automatically to the seaward side of the *Minerva*, leaning over the rail to catch what little fresh breeze there was.

Below her, the sea moved rhythmically against the pristine white paintwork, soothing, lulling. It would be so easy to allow herself to give in to the way she felt about Luke, as easy as it would be to give in to the insidious pull of the sea. All she had to do was to close her eyes and let her body . . .

'Gemma! What the hell do you think you're doing?'

Hard hands jerked her back from the rail, swinging her round and dropping her on to the deck. The shock of it jolted right through her, her eyes opening on to Luke's grim face.

'I was just watching the sea.' She rubbed at the painful spots on her arms where he had held her.

'Watching it? Like hell! You were leaning over so far, another roll of the boat would have had you over. Is that what you were trying to do? Death before dishonour?'

That ugly, bitter sound was back in his voice, and she went to him instinctively, hating herself for being responsible for putting it there, placing her fingers against his lips. They felt warm and hard, sending tiny electric tingles racing through her skin.

'Luke, you're being ridiculous. I came up here for some air. Perhaps I was leaning over too far, but that's all it was, I promise you. I don't consider making love with you as "dishonour", you know that.'

The insults and snubs of his early years had scarred him much more deeply than she had known.

'Perhaps I was over-reacting. Guilt, I expect.' He grimaced slightly. 'You've always had such a quality of untouched purity about you. Even as a child you had it; the security of wealthy parents who can afford to shield their children from reality.'

'Not always. Just think how many sons and daughters of wealthy parents abuse themselves with drugs.'

'Your parents didn't want you to come out here with me,' he said, abruptly changing track.

'My parents don't make any decisions for me, Luke.'

'So it isn't because of them that you ...'

'Don't want us to be lovers?' She was standing so close to him that she could see the tiny lines raying out from his eyes. He moved slightly and in the yacht's dimmed lights she saw that he was barefoot.

As he followed her gaze down his body he said drily, 'I saw you up here just after I came out of the shower.'

Gemma's skin burned suddenly as she realised that the jeans he was wearing were damp in places, obviously from his skin. He had pulled on a shirt, but it wasn't fastened, and the clean scent of his body was doing odd things to her pulse rate.

'I should have been honest with you right from the start,' he said wryly.

If he had been, would she have come out here with him? she wondered.

'Instead . . .'

'Instead, you decided it was a case of once aboard the lugger, and the girl is mine,' Gemma teased lightly, her sense of humour suddenly surfacing.

He laughed. 'Now you're insulting me, Gemma; nothing as obvious as that, I assure you. You've always been able to make me laugh,' he added on a more sombre note. 'I think you're the only woman I know I like and respect as a person almost as much as I desire you.'

Yes, Gemma could sense that. Luke didn't want any woman to get too close to him, so he kept his respect and friendship for those he didn't desire, and chose only to take to his bed those with whom he knew there would be no cerebral contact.

Now wasn't the time to ask why he was so anti-commitment, and besides, she suspected she already knew the answer. She remembered that she had once asked him about his parents, and he had told her that his mother had married beneath her and that she had deserted her husband and son when Luke was three years old.

His father had been a car mechanic, forced to leave his son shut up in his bedroom during the day while he was out at work, because he could not afford to pay anyone to look after him.

One day his father had suffered an accident at work and had been taken to hospital, where he fell into a coma and eventually died, but it had been three days before a neighbour decided to investigate the noises from the supposedly empty house, and had discovered the terrified three-year-old, locked in his room for safety by a father who had feared to allow him the run of the house in case he touched the cooker or a fire.

The social services people had tracked down Luke's mother, but she had refused to take charge of the child. She wanted to forget all about her marriage and her son, so Luke had been taken into care.

Deep down inside, he probably still distrusted people, Gemma suspected, and that was why he refused to commit himself to a relationship.

She suspected that he was probably more relaxed and forthcoming with her than he was with other people because of their earlier friendship. A special bond had been forged between them then that nothing could break: a bond that had enabled her to trust him enough to ask him to teach her how to kiss; a bond that had been strong enough for him to do so without taking advantage of her innocence and inexperience.

But now they were adult, and Luke still wanted her. She touched his face again with gentle fingers and felt him tense as he growled hoarsely, 'For God's sake,

Gemma, I'm not an emotionless computer. Touch me like that, and I'm going to react. In fact, touch me at all, and I'm going to react,' he admitted frankly, making her shiver with reciprocal desire, and even though she knew she was doing the very thing she should not, Gemma moved closer to him, placing her hands on the smooth flesh of his shoulders.

'Gemma.' She could feel the sound of his groan moving his chest as her fingertips automatically smoothed the exciting heat of his skin. She bent her head and touched her lips to his throat, not knowing until that moment just how much she had wanted to touch him like that. Beneath her mouth she felt the rigid movement of his muscles.

'Gemma.' His voice was harsh with tension. She knew that she should stop, that she was doing something that was both wrong and dangerous, but the huge yellow moon and the soft sighing of the sea against the hull of the yacht wove a spell around her that she didn't want to break.

Just one kiss, she told herself; just one kiss would harm neither of them, but when it came and Luke's mouth opened over hers in famished, passionate need, she knew that she was wrong and that she would be hurt.

But it was too late to stop even if her body had let her, and so instead she gave herself up to the voluptuous heat flooding through her body, opening her lips to the demanding thrust of Luke's tongue as it mirrored the fierce movement of his hips against her body.

She had had no idea that a kiss could be so sexual, that she could feel this savage clawing need to be closer and closer to him, to want to absorb him completely within her.

There was no thought in her mind of holding back. She welcomed the heat of his hand beneath her blouse as he caressed the fullness of her breast. His thumb stroked the hard point of her nipple and beneath his mouth she cried out in pleasure. One of them was shaking . . . *both* of them were shaking, she acknowledged. And then, so abruptly that she could hardly credit it, Luke was pushing her away from him.

'They're changing the watch,' he told her thickly. 'Come down to my cabin, Gemma.'

God, how she wanted to go with him, but now that he had stopped touching her, sanity flooded back. If he made love to her . . . If he made love to her he would bind her to him even more. She would be desperately hurt when the time eventually came when he grew bored with her. She didn't think she had the strength to endure that sort of pain. No, it was better to call a halt now.

'I'm sorry, Luke, I can't do that.'

She could have wept for the expression of pain and bitterness in his eyes, but it was too late to call back the words, even if she had wantd to.

'I suppose I should have expected that. What happened, an attack of conscience? Remembered Hardman, did you?'

Gemma didn't answer, seizing on the escape avenue he had given her. If he thought that she and Tom Hardman were more than mere acquaintances then . . .

'I should have taken you here on the deck,' he sneered nastily. 'You were certainly willing enough to let me. More than willing.'

Gemma felt her face burn, but she couldn't deny that he was right. She had wanted him to make love to her, had invited it, in fact, so she bowed her head beneath the painful lash of his scorn.

Several yards away she heard the murmur of male voices as the watch changed. She couldn't endure any more, not tonight. Unable to say a word, she whirled round and headed for the companionway, knowing without turning round that Luke was standing watching her.

Alone in her room she tore off her clothes. Her breasts still ached, missing the pleasure of Luke's caress, and there was a restless, almost painful need coiling in her lower stomach.

She ought to have let well alone. Now she had only made things worse. She sensed that Luke would not allow her to break her contract, and she certainly could not afford to pay the penalty sum of three months' wages, if she broke it without his agreement. She had thought at the time it was an odd clause to insert, but Luke had pointed out to her that, with so many of his staff coming from Britain, he had to ensure that they did not let him down half-way through a project. She was here and here she would have to stay.

She was tempted to find hotel accommodation, but it would be expensive, and she had very little cash. Her arrangement with Luke was that she would be paid in a lump sum once her contract was completed.

She was trapped, more by her own folly than by Luke's machinations. If she had only let things be and not kissed him . . . But she had, and now it was too late, because once having tasted his mouth, having known that sweetly fierce surge of desire and need that he had aroused within her, she wasn't sure that she would be able to stop herself from wanting more.

If she had merely desired him sexually it would have been bad enough, but she was very much afraid that she loved him as well, and had perhaps always done so. Certainly it would explain why no one else had ever been able to penetrate the protective aura of reserve she wrapped around herself. Mentally she had obviously always been comparing them to Luke, and finding them wanting, even if she hadn't been prepared to admit as much before.

She remembered quite startlingly how disappointed she had been by Tom's kiss, and the desolation with which she had compared it to Luke's. The warning signs had been there then, but she had been too young and ignorant to translate them. The seeds of her love for him had been there all the time, waiting for the right moment to germinate into adult love. Now that moment was here, and she suspected there wasn't a single thing she could do to stop her love for him from going on growing and growing.

After a restless night, Gemma went on deck heavy eyed with tension and trepidation, only to discover that Luke had already left for the site, and that, what was more, he had left instructions for her to be taken over to the shore where the personnel officer would pick her up, and then take her round to meet the men.

There was no suggestion in his message of any degree of personal interest or desire. She could have quite genuinely been nothing more than his employee. She ought to have felt relieved, but instead ... instead she felt let down and edgy, she admitted, as she toyed with the breakfast the steward brought her, unable to face even the delicious fresh fruit that had been prepared for her.

By the time she had finished her second cup of coffee she was feeling a little more robust. If Luke could be indifferent and distant, then so could she.

She dressed in a very workmanlike all-in-one peach cotton jumpsuit for her visit to the site, adding soft cotton boots, sunglasses and a sunhat.

When she was convinced that she looked as business-like as possible she checked her canvas shoulder bag to make sure that she had notebooks and pencils, and then went up on deck to find someone to take her across in the launch.

As promised, Harry Barker was waiting for her. He greeted her with a brief smile, and now Gemma had no difficulty at all in interpreting the sidelong look he gave her. Of course, he and the others were all wondering about her relationship with Luke. Thank goodness her sunglasses hid the evidence of her broken night, otherwise he might put an interpretation of an entirely different and erroneous sort on the dark circles beneath her eyes.

As they got into the buggy he had parked by the jetty, he eyed her sunhat with a frown and reached behind her to produce a bright red safety helmet with the words 'O'Rourke Constructions' printed on it in white.

'The boss said to make sure that you wore this.'

He paused as though expecting her to demur. It certainly clashed with her hair and her clothes, Gemma thought wryly, but she knew the safety rules operating on construction sites, and the reasons behind them, and she wasn't about to argue.

'Thanks,' she said casually, taking it from him with a smile and exchanging it for her sunhat. It felt oppressively hot after the lightweight straw, and within seconds of putting it on she could feel the beads of sweat breaking out on her scalp, but she wasn't going to give in. She was here to do a job, and she meant to do that job well.

It was hard, far harder than she had envisaged, to keep her mind on the men she was meeting and off Luke, but somehow she managed it, and by the time Harry Barker insisted on a brief break, her mind was teeming with information and impressions.

The men—well, boys really—to whom she had talked, were all so eager to learn that they had fired her own enthusiasm. Luke was already providing on-the-job technical training, but it was the formal, educational knowledge behind that training that they needed so badly if they were ever to go out into the world and work elsewhere.

It hadn't taken her long to discover how much all of them respected and admired Luke. There seemed to be no aspect of their lives he was not concerned in, from the establishment of a health clinic that was free to all his employees and their families, right down to crèche facilities for the women who worked in the site canteen.

The people of St George's might be poor, but they were proud and independent; they respected what Luke had done with his life, and they trusted him, Gemma realised.

She had her meal in the works canteen alongside the men, and then afterwards she was given a tour of the immaculate kitchens.

'One of the main problems we have with the locals is that they are inclined to be very much "come a day go a day",' Ian Cameron, the burly Scot explained to her when he joined them. 'For many of them, while they can grow a few greens and keep a few fowl, they can't see any need for anything else.'

'Well, there's a lot to be said for being content with one's life,' Gemma pointed out.

'Ay, just as long as they're allowed to live that life. Very few of them own their own land outright.' He frowned suddenly and looked at his watch. 'I forgot, the boss said to take you along to his office after you'd eaten.'

'The boss'. How well that appellation fitted Luke. He wore the mantle of authority and responsibility well. His men trusted him; just as she had trusted him, she remembered, leaning on him and drawing strength from his maturity. Intrinsically he was still that same Luke, despite the sophistication and the cool accentless voice, and surely she could still trust him?

But in what context? As a friend, as one human being to another, yes, but as a man ... as a lover ...

She was being unfair to him, Gemma told herself. She could trust him as far as the limits he put around his relationship with her sex; it was just that those limits were too narrow to control her own emotions.

She stiffened abruptly, staring into space, not seeing the puzzled look Ian Cameron gave her.

'The office is this way.' He touched her arm lightly, and Gemma shook off the feeling of shock weakening

her body, numbly following his lead as they skirted
foundations and plant, and headed for one of the
Portacabins. It was frighteningly disconcerting to realise
how vulnerable her love for him made her. She only had
to think about him and she became deaf, dumb and blind
to everything else.

Ian Cameron and Harry Barker stopped outside the
Portacabin door, and rapped on it. Gemma heard Luke's
voice call out curtly, 'Come . . .' and then Ian Cameron
was pushing her gently towards the open door, leaving
her alone with Luke, Gemma realised, whilst her heart
jolted crazily like a rubber ball bouncing on a string.

CHAPTER NINE

ONLY they weren't alone. Someone else was in the cabin with them; someone else who leaned so close to Luke's hard shoulder that he must be aware of the full curve of her breast pressed against his body, of the musky essence of her perfume, because she could smell it from where she stood, Gemma thought miserably, averting her eyes from the sight of Samantha clinging possessively to Luke's side.

'I'm sorry, I didn't realise you weren't alone.'

What on earth was she apologising for? Luke had sent for her, after all.

She saw the triumph flare in Samantha's eyes, and felt the earth rock slightly beneath her feet with the shock of the white-hot stab of jealousy that tore through her.

She had never experienced such primitive emotion before, and it almost tore her apart with its violence. That such an intensity of feeling could be aroused by something as simple as the fact that Samantha was leaning possessively against Luke's body made Gemma realise how much she must love him. They were so alien to her previous experience, these charged, desperate feelings, and she wanted to turn away from them, just as she wanted to turn and run away from Luke, she acknowledged.

'Samantha was just leaving,' Luke told her, disengaging himself from the other woman's grasp with fluid ease and walking across the small hut to hold open the door for her.

When she saw that she had no alternative but to go, Samantha pouted slightly at him, protesting, 'But Luke, you haven't given me your answer.'

'You can tell your uncle that I'll be in touch.'

Gemma didn't want to turn round and look at them, so instead she studied the maps and plans pinned to the walls, trying desperately to pretend that she was too fascinated by them to be aware of Samantha's pouting protests, or Luke's responses to them.

The other woman was a trier, she recognised, or had Luke had a change of heart and decided to reinstate their relationship?

The icy chill that ran through her veins at the thought of Luke with any other woman frightened her, the pain holding her in its fierce grip was such that she almost thought she might faint. In fact, the cabin *was* starting to sway around her in a decidedly odd fashion, and she reached instinctively to remove her hot, confining helmet, a small tortured sound of panic escaping from her throat as she fought to escape the waves of nausea and darkness sucking her down into their depths.

From behind her she heard the door close, and then Luke's sharp exclamation. She was aware of falling, falling frighteningly fast, as in the very worst kind of nightmare, and then there was only comfort and warmth, a sense of peace and security that she accepted and clung to gratefully, unaware that it was Luke to whom she clung, who caught her just before she collapsed, and who quickly carried her over to the makeshift narrow bunk he used on those occasions when he was required to stay overnight at the site.

'Gemma.'

She didn't try to open her eyes, but focused all her inner attention on Luke's voice.

'Don't try to move. You fainted. Heat shock, I suspect.' Suddenly his voice sounded very grim, and Gemma wondered if he was having second thoughts about her suitability for her job. As much as she had wanted to leave the island when he told her he wanted to sleep with her, she now wanted to stay. Recklessly she admitted to herself that she wanted him on any terms he was prepared to make. After all, how many women ever had even as much as she would have if she and Luke were lovers?

It was high time she joined the twentieth century and accepted that life did not come guaranteed with happy ever afters. Luke wanted her . . . he had told her so. Let that be enough. From somewhere she would find the strength to blot out the future, to live only for the present, to take each day, each hour she had with him and savour them. Somehow she would keep her secret from him, would hide from him the fact that she loved him. She owed both him and herself that.

She opened her eyes and looked directly at him. He was frowning, deep creases scoring the tanned planes of his face. He looked older, sterner. Her whole body ached with yearning for him. She reached up and touched his face with trembling fingers, her eyes widening with shock and pain as he suddenly jerked back as though her touch burned like acid.

'Luke.'

He ignored her soft protest, saying harshly, 'I've got

to get you back to the yacht. You're obviously not properly acclimatised yet.'

Had he recoiled from her touch because he no longer wanted her? It was frustrating to realise that she knew so little about the actuality of male sexuality that she had no way of gauging how intense or otherwise his desire for her might be. Luke was adept at concealing his deeper feelings; he had learned how to do so in an extremely hard school ... But he *must* still want her, she thought frantically. He had told her only last night that he did.

Round and round her tortured thoughts pursued one another while Luke reached for the phone and gave several harsh commands into the receiver. When he replaced it he looked at her.

'The launch is coming across to pick you up.'

Her ears were so finely attuned to all the subtle nuances of his voice that she picked it up immediately, and repeated questioningly, 'To pick *me* up? Aren't you coming with me?'

'I've got work to do, Gemma.' How harsh and uncompromising his voice was. 'I can't play nursemaid to you. I warned you about overdoing things.'

'Yes, and then you insisted that I wear a safety helmet, almost guaranteed to fry the inside of my head,' she protested bitterly.

'When you're on a building site you have to abide by the safety rules ... you know that. Or didn't *Daddy* ever let his delicate little daughter go near any of the places that earned the money that sent her to that exclusive girls' school, and paid for that nice house in the country?'

God, what was happening to them? They were on the

verge of quarrelling. Luke was deliberately trying to hurt her. She couldn't believe it. She *wouldn't* believe it.

'Luke, please . . .'

He hesitated, his eyes betraying the fact that he was torn by conflicting emotions. He did still want her, Gemma recognised, but something was holding him back, stopping him from coming to her. Unashamedly she held out her arms, but to her hurt dismay he turned away from her, clamping the muscles in his jaw so that she caught the betraying movement as he turned away from her and strode over to the door, flinging it open.

'Ray,' Gemma heard him shout. 'I want you to escort Miss Parish down to the launch. Keep an eye on her,' he warned the young coffee-coloured boy who came into the cabin. 'She's suffering from heatstroke.'

The boy was one of those Gemma had talked to earlier. She recognised him and forced herself to smile at him. After all, it wasn't his fault that Luke had chosen to reject her.

Luke had rejected her. The words hammered at her heart and pulse points all the way back to the yacht. She felt sick inside, and dreadfully weak and shaky, but it wasn't heatstroke that was bothering her, she was sure. More like emotional exhaustion, a complete inability to face up to and deal with the fact that, having said he wanted her, Luke had apparently now decided to control that wanting and turn away from her.

But Luke was a very sexual man. Jealousy hit her like the tip of a knife inserted skilfully and deliberately just below the heart. She could feel the pain of it bursting inside her. She wanted to scream and rage against it, but all she could do was make tiny whimpers of pain and misery into the softness of her pillow.

Every time she closed her eyes, the luxury of her cabin faded away and she was tortured by mental images of Samantha with Luke, of their bodies entwined, of Luke caressing her skin.

Sweat was pouring off her own body, but she felt too weak to get up and take a shower.

Muddled, confused images from the past mingled with those from the present.

Gemma slept fitfully, constantly being woken either by rigours of icy cold shivering, or dreadful hot sweats. Occasionally she was aware of someone else in the cabin, touching her fevered skin, proffering cool drinks, talking to her and soothing her, but she pushed them away, knowing instinctively that the competent hands did not belong to the one she wanted.

It was dark when she was woken by the low murmur of voices beside her bed. Her eyelids were far too heavy for her to lift, but she could hear the whispered conversation.

'It's heatstroke all right, and she's had a bad bout of it.'

'I told you I didn't want to be disturbed.'

That was Luke's voice. Gemma wanted to call out to him, but she simply didn't have the strength.

'I know that, sir, but she kept calling out for you.' The captain ... The captain had heard her calling out for Luke. She could feel the embarrassed colour stinging her skin.

'Her temperature's come down now, and she's through the worst of it.'

'But you still disturbed me, despite my orders to the

contrary. Why was that, I wonder, Captain?'

Gemma wondered as well, but she wasn't privileged to see the look that passed between the captain and Luke. The captain had a vast experience of human nature, and Luke O'Rourke was a man he admired more than anyone else he had ever worked for, but like all men he was only human.

'You're wrong, Captain,' Gemma heard him saying savagely after a long gap. 'The weakness is mine, not hers, and my absence ... my absence was born of the purest of all man's emotions.'

Gemma was too exhausted to puzzle out what Luke meant by those cryptic words. All she really cared about was the fact that he was here at her side.

She reached out her hand, and managed to croak his name.

'Yes, I'm here, Gemma. Now try to go to sleep. You're all right ... now.'

Yes she was, because now Luke was here. She closed her eyes and slid into sleep.

When she opened them again it was still dark. She felt remarkably clear-headed, and grimaced wryly as she glanced at her watch and saw that it was only half past two in the morning.

As she lay awake she heard the watch changing duty but for once the rhythmic roll of the yacht failed to lull her into sleep.

She wanted to be with Luke, she acknowledged. She wanted to be held in his arms, to be close to him in every way there was. She wanted him, she admitted, and that wanting got worse by the moment.

The captain, or whoever else had tended her when she

was ill, had put her to bed in her underwear, she suddenly realised. Her skin felt gritty and uncomfortable, the nagging ache of desire deep down in her body refusing to go away.

Restlessly she got up and paced her cabin. She needed a shower, or perhaps even better a warm bath. That might help relax her.

Only it didn't. As she soaped her skin she was aware of her body in a way she had never been before, and as she dried herself on one of the huge fluffy towels, she couldn't help wondering what it would be like if Luke was touching her ... caressing her.

She dropped the towel and stood motionless. There was only one way to find out. Her heart was beating very, very fast, but outwardly she looked totally composed and in control.

Somewhere she had a thick towelling robe. Where was it? She found it eventually and pulled it on. If any of the crew should see her ... They would have to draw their own conclusions, she told herself hardily; after all, she was a woman, not a child.

She knew where Luke's suite was, of course, and as she hurried silently towards it, she sent up a little prayer that he had not returned to the site.

The handle turned easily, the door swinging noiselessly inwards as she hurried into the sitting-room as silently as a pale moth.

Everything was in darkness, but there was enough light for her to see where she was going from the moonlight outside.

She had reached the door to Luke's bedroom. She paused outside it, her heart hammering.

The door opened inwards. She held her breath as she stepped inside and saw the figure lying on the bed. Luke was here. He moved and she froze, but he was still asleep, one arm flung out across the bed, the brown tanned length of his back exposed where the bedclothes had slid away.

Her heart was thumping so loudly that Gemma felt sure it must wake him. She closed the door gently and made her way round to the far side of the bed. Luke slept facing not the door, but the porthole, and a silvery beam of moonlight highlighted the hard angles of his face. Shivering with fear and anticipation, Gemma only just managed to resist tracing the jutting outline of one hard cheekbone where the light slanted across it, knowing that if she touched him he might wake up, and she was still not ready.

It was too late now for second thoughts, she told herself. She had come here because she wanted Luke to make love to her. If she left now, she would spend the rest of her life regretting her cowardice.

She took a deep breath, and unfastened the tie of her robe, shrugging it of her shoulders so that it fell at her feet in a pool of white cloth.

Just for a moment she stood there, trembling violently in a mixture of apprehension and excitement. Tiny goosebumps of flesh studded her skin, the moonlight gilding her flesh palest silver, and then she moved, lifting back the covers.

Suddenly her control deserted her, and she scrambled into the bed alongside him as awkwardly and as nervously as a small child escaping from its night-time demons.

His skin was warm, the male scent of him clinging to the air. He moved, opened his eyes, and then tensed as he saw her.

'Gemma?' There was no uncertainty in his voice, only grim comprehension. 'What . . .'

She touched her fingers to his lips and shook her head, her eyes pleading for the understanding she was still too shy to voice.

And then, when she had commanded his silence, she touched his face with tender loving fingertips, willing him to understand all that she could not say, fighting to stop herself from drowning in the intensity of her own desire as she felt the hard warmness of his skin against her own.

'Gemma . . . for God's sake.' He moved restlessly, and a thrill of awareness shocked through her as she felt the arousal of his body. He wanted her . . . he did want her. It was all the encouragement she needed.

'Luke, make love to me. Please make love to me.' She raised her face to his, her lips trembling against the hard planes of his face, breathing in the scent of his skin, and loving the faint rasp that was the beginning of his beard as he smothered a harsh sound of protest, and found her mouth with his own.

It was like drowning, dying, and being re-born; it was all the pleasure she had ever imagined existed and then some more. The simple act of fusing her mouth with his brought her such delight that she thought she might die from it.

Her hands lifted to his shoulders, savouring their warm silk texture, her body straining eagerly against his, her sensitive nipples hardening as they felt the heat and strength of his chest.

'Gemma, for heaven's sake!'

'I want you.' She said it fiercely, obliterating his shaken whisper, knowing with an instinct that went beyond mere knowledge that he was fighting against wanting her, that he was going to send her away. Only she wasn't going to let him.

She twined her arms round his neck and pressed herself wantonly against him, feeling the shudder of desire tense his body.

'You taught me how to kiss, Luke ... now teach me how to make love.' She whispered the words against his mouth, and felt his reaction to them in the way his body tensed.

'My God, you really know how to turn a man on, don't you? I'd have to be a saint to resist an invitation like that. What's happened, Gemma?' he demanded broodingly. 'Why have you changed your mind?'

She couldn't answer that question, and so instead she rubbed herself sinuously against him with an abandonment that would make her cringe with embarrassment later, no doubt, but which now brought a harsh cry of pleasure from Luke's throat, and made her own body tinglingly aware of how delicious just the mere contact of flesh against flesh could be.

'Gemma, we shouldn't be doing this.'

'Yes, we should.' Her nails dug tormentingly into his skin as she pressed her mouth against his throat, tasting the salty male flavour of it.

'My God ... What the hell are you trying to do to me?'

'Make you want me as much as I want you.'

He couldn't stop himself from reacting to her words. She felt the unmistakable surge of his body against hers, and knew with exultation that she had won.

'Oh, Gemma, I've dreamed of making love to you so many many times, but never, ever did I dream it would be like this. That you would be the one seducing me.'

He muttered something else, but the words were lost against her skin as his mouth plundered the tender curve of her throat, sucking and biting on her soft skin until she was shivering with a pleasure that reached right down to her toes.

Her inexperience, her lack of sexual expertise, were forgotten as she responded blindly to the inflammatory combination of his touch and her desire. Wherever his hand and mouth touched her, her skin burned, her body melting with heat and pleasure.

His hands found her breasts, cupping their soft roundness, and she moaned with pleasure. His thumbs stroked the tight hardness of her nipples and she smothered the cry of need that rose into her throat by pressing her mouth into his shoulder. It was only when he shuddered against her that Gemma realised that she had bitten him. Her body flushed with shame until she heard him saying hoarsely, 'Oh, God, Gemma, you want me as much as I want you, don't you? Don't you?' he demanded thickly, rolling her over so that she was lying on her back and he was looking down into the vulnerable oval of her face.

She didn't need to say anything; her face and body gave her away.

'I've waited so long . . . so long for this. I'm going to enjoy every second of it. We both are,' he told her softly, and Gemma was surprised that he couldn't actually see the frantic kick of her heartbeat as he bent his head and delicately anointed the pointed thrust of one breast with the moist heat of his tongue.

It was pleasure almost beyond bearing, a wild symphony of delight that transcended mortality and lifted her into the realms of the gods.

Her body arched in eager supplication, her eyes glazed with desire as they fastened on his.

'You liked that?' Her expression gave her away. 'You're so responsive to my mouth. What will you be like when I taste the secrets of your womanhood, Gemma?'

She couldn't stop the shudder of reaction that ran through her, and, as though he knew exactly what she was feeling, Luke bent his head again and deliberately took her nipple into his mouth, caressing it slowly until she felt she was going to go mad with need.

In the silver moonlight, her body was arched up to him like a pagan offering. She hadn't even realised that he had thrust back the bedclothes until she felt his hands on her waist and she looked down and saw the naked arch of her torso.

'Perfect . . . so perfect that you make me ache . . . Did you know that, Gemma?'

His hand slid down to caress the thrust of her hip, and lingered darkly against her slim thigh, his thumb slowly probing its soft inner curve, until she shivered feverishly, her body going weak and boneless, melting in the tremendous heat burning inside her.

'Luke . . .'

'Shush . . .' He was leaning over her, looking at her,

and wantonly she felt herself respond to that look, aching for him ... wanting him ...

'Gemma!'

Her name burst from his throat on a tortured moan of male need. His mouth captured her other nipple, not gently this time, but fiercely, wantingly, sucking and tugging on its swollen hardness until she could hardly bear the waves of sensation beating through her.

Distantly she was aware of calling out his name, of her feverish response to the sensation of his hand stroking between her thighs as surge after surge of pleasure shocked through her, and she clung desperately to him, unable to do anything other than scatter pleading kisses against his skin and hope that she could somehow ride out the sensual storm battering her.

'You're so soft ... so moist ... I want to touch and taste all of you, Gemma. All of you.'

She heard him moan the plea against her mouth as it parted to admit the thrust of his tongue, but its meaning was lost as his hands skimmed her body, stroking, coaxing, arousing, until she was on fire for him, aching for him to take her and make her completely his.

When he moved, and she felt the absence of the hard abrasion of his hair-roughened chest against her own, she cried out, reaching for him, her fingers curling into his dark hair as he pushed her back against the bed and slid his hands beneath her hips so that he could lift her and caress the soft, quivering female centre of her with the moist heat of his mouth and tongue, until ripples of pleasure burned through her and her fingers relaxed their shocked grip of his hair and her body writhed in a paroxysm of delight so intense that she didn't know how she could bear it.

While her body was still enjoying it, Luke moved, taking her into his arms.

'I wanted that so badly, Gemma. I've dreamed of it so often, seeing you abandoned to pleasure in my arms. Feel what you're doing to me.'

He moved slowly, entering her with what she knew instinctively was finesse and skill, but even so there was still a brief shock of pain to make her muscles tense, and her eyes dilate.

Any hopes she had had that Luke wouldn't realise that she was still a virgin were lost as she looked into his eyes, but it was too late for him to stop and withdraw; his body was as lost to his control as hers had been earlier. As he surged within her, she heard him curse and try to tense, but the pain was gone, and in its place was the faint echo of the pleasure she had known before, so she clung to him, letting her body adapt to the intimacy of his within it, letting her senses and her love guide her as the echo grew stronger, until she was able to move eagerly against him, and feel the triumphant climactic surge of pleasure spiral through her as he moved faster, deeper, taking them both free of man's limited boundaries.

'Gemma!'

She heard him cry out her name as pleasure exploded inside her, as he moaned his satisfaction into her throat, sending an extra thrill of emotion down her spine. There was something so primitive, so satisfying, about knowing that he had achieved the highest pinnacle of male satisfaction within her, that in that moment she didn't even care that their union might result in her conceiving.

All she cared about was Luke. Luke whom she loved. Luke who had given her such pleasure ... who had finally shown her why she had never wanted anyone else as her lover.

'Gemma.'

She murmured sleepily, curling into his body, a soft, satiated smile curling her mouth, unaware that he was looking down at her with a frown, or that he lay tense and sleepless for a long, long time before giving in to the relentless urging of his flesh that he take her into his arms, and enjoy the delight of holding her naked body next to his own.

CHAPTER TEN

'GEMMA ... Gemma, wake up.'

The harsh sound of Luke's voice jarred through the sleepy daze engulfing her. Reluctantly Gemma opened her eyes, stretching her body in languorous pleasure. She felt so good, so relaxed, and yet so ... so womanly. She almost wanted to purr. A ripple of amused pleasure ran down her spine, quickly changing to tense apprehension as she looked up and saw the grimness in Luke's eyes.

'You'd better get back to your room before the steward comes in with my breakfast,' Luke told her coldly. 'Here.'

He clambered out of bed, long-limbed, and so male that she could feel a reactionary shudder rippling through her sensitive flesh. There were faint dark bruises on his shoulder, and marks on his back, she saw as he turned round to pick up her discarded robe. Marks that she had left there last night.

She moved restlessly beneath the bedclothes, her breasts a little tender. If she closed her eyes she could still remember what it felt like to have Luke's mouth ...

'Gemma!'

She couldn't endure the icy bitterness in his eyes.

'Luke, please, what is it? What have I done ... said?'

'It's rather what you haven't said,' he told her in a clipped voice. 'Why didn't you tell me you were a virgin?'

He was angry because of *that*. But why? Suddenly she knew. Luke thought that she might use her virginity as a means of trapping him into a commitment he could not give her. It hurt unbearably that he could think that, that he could not see that her body, like her love, was given freely. Numb with pain, she demanded listlessly,

'How? It isn't exactly the sort of thing one talks about. What ought I to have done? Hired a billboard?'

'Don't be so bloody ridiculous,' he said roughly.

He was still standing holding her robe, and suddenly Gemma knew she had to get out of his room or betray herself completely by bursting into tears and telling him that she loved him.

She pushed back the covers and snatched her robe from him, pulling it on with her back to him. 'I'm sorry if the fact that I was a virgin disappointed you,' she said tightly, adding with a bitter twist of her mouth, 'At least it won't happen again.'

There was a tense pause and then Luke said fiercely, 'You're damned right it won't. I don't like being used, although I suppose I should be used to it—from you.'

It was a dig at her adolescent plea all those years ago, and it was enough to send the colour scorching fiercely along her veins.

Tears stung her eyes, pain flooding her as she said huskily, 'I'm sorry if I don't have Samantha's experience.'

'At least Samantha is honest about what she wants,' Luke came back harshly.

It was too much: to be compared with Samantha and to be found wanting. Her eyes bright with tears, Gemma ran to the door. She could hear Luke calling her back as she fled, but she didn't stop until she was back in her own suite, and even then taking the precaution of locking herself in her bathroom, and then running the taps full force so that the sound of the running water obliterated the sound of the sobs of anguish torn from her throat. So much for being adult! She was behaving like a lovelorn teenager. But the pain wouldn't stop, going on and on, and it was no use telling herself that it was her own fault, that Luke had not invited her into his bed, and that she had known all along that all he felt for her was desire.

She cringed now to remember her abandoned response to him. How amused he must have been by her naïveté.

But he hadn't known she had no previous experience until his body told him so, she remembered now. Surely a man of his sexual expertise must have realised long before that how untutored she was. But then her reaction to him had been so passionate . . . so wanton . . .

Long after her tears had stopped, she remained locked in her bathroom, bathing her eyes in pads soaked in cold water. She heard Luke calling her name outside the bathroom door and tensed.

'Gemma. Are you all right?'

How galling that he should feel it necessary to ask her that. He must know how much he had hurt her. How stupid she had been.

Compressing her lips she called back curtly. 'I'm fine, Luke. Please go away.'

It seemed to be a long time before she heard him move; so long that her lungs ached from the strain of holding her breath.

She had rushed into the bathroom with nothing but the robe she had been wearing, and she put it on again, cautiously studying her pale face in the mirror before reaching for the door handle.

She looked pale, but then that was only to be expected after her attack of heatstroke. Luckily she could wear sunglasses during the day to hide her eyes, which still looked slightly puffy.

She opened the bathroom door and walked into her bedroom, coming to an abrupt halt as she saw Luke sitting in a chair, his arms folded over his chest.

'Luke.'

She stared at him, flushing betrayingly, her eyes unknowingly wide and vulnerable.

'I thought . . .'

'That I'd left?'

He looked grimly at her. 'You might have made me angry enough to behave like a callow boy, Gemma, but I'm not one. Are you all right? Physically, I meant,' he added bluntly in a softer voice, not allowing her to drag her embarrassed gaze from his.

'Last night. Well, I didn't realise you were still a virgin. If I had . . .'

'If you had you wouldn't have come anywhere near me,' Gemma supplied tautly. 'I'm not made of glass, Luke, even if twenty-four is a rather advanced age to . . . to have sex for the first time.'

'For God's sake!' He shot up, and frowned darkly at her. 'To have sex . . .' His mouth twisted. 'You make it sound like taking nasty medicine, and we both know that it wasn't like that, don't we, Gemma?'

Was she imagining that hint of pleading in his voice? She must be, Gemma reasoned, because there was nothing remotely pleading about the look he was giving her.

'I don't know what you mean.'

What ridiculous bravado had made her say that?

'Like hell you don't. You know exactly what I mean. You and I didn't have sex, Gemma, we gave and took enjoyment and pleasure, in equal measures, and if you try to deny it then I'll damn well prove to you here and now that you're lying.'

Gemma froze. What was he saying?

Panic flared through her body, and she automatically stepped back from him.

'Luke, I'm leaving . . . just as soon as a flight can be arranged.' She couldn't stay here now. Not now, when he had just shown her how contemptuous of her he was.

A dark tide of colour ran up under his skin as he came towards her. 'Running back to Hardman are you, just like you did once before, to show him what you've learned in my arms? Of course he's much more your type than I am, isn't he, Gemma? Much more acceptable to Mummy and Daddy. I'm good enough to teach you how to use that beautiful body of yours, but I'm not good enough for anything else. Is that it?'

He was still coming towards her, and Gemma had an insane desire to giggle. It was tension, she told herself, that was all. Luke couldn't possibly mean what he was saying. He knew that she loved him. Didn't he? He didn't look as though he did, Gemma thought wryly. He looked absolutely furious, and . . . A fine flicker of excitement burned through her veins as she looked at him properly and saw past his anger to the fierce desire glittering in his eyes.

He wanted her. He still wanted her. She felt her senses catch fire, and murmured his name, but he thought she was denying him and said thickly. 'Well, perhaps before you go running back to Hardman I'd better just complete your education for you. I'd hate to think I'd missed out on anything,' he added nastily, desire surmounted by the raging bitterness she saw in his eyes.

For the first time fear touched her. This wasn't the Luke she knew and loved. She had to explain.

'Luke, please stop,' she begged. 'You don't understand. You . . .'

'No, you're the one who doesn't understand,' he corrected harshly. 'You never have done. Oh, no, Gemma, I'm not letting you walk away from me this time. Before, I had to. Legally you were a child, but now you're a woman and there's nothing to stop me from showing you what being a woman is all about.'

'You already have,' Gemma told him tartly, both angry and afraid. It didn't help that she knew that she had brought some of his anger down upon her own head, but it was too late to reason and argue. Implacable determination showed in every movement of his supple body. He was stalking her like an animal stalking its prey, she recognised helplessly, measuring the distance to the bathroom door, and knowing she wouldn't make it.

'Run all you like, Gemma,' he taunted her. 'You won't get very far.'

He was practically hypnotising her with his eyes. Gemma thought wildly, making it impossible for her to move, to do anything other than stand there trembling like a trapped doe while he came towards her. He reached out and circled one delicate wrist with his fingers, tugging her gently towards him.

'Stop shaking,' he whispered against her ear. 'There's nothing to be frightened of.'

He was lying. She knew that. Oh he wouldn't hurt her physically—he wasn't that sort of man—but emotionally . . . She was too vulnerable, too deeply in love with him to be able to protect herself against him.

Perhaps if she told him? But no, she couldn't do that. She couldn't betray that final humiliating weakness. Somehow she would just have to find a way of physically resisting him. But how?

It was a question she was to ask herself over and over again in the moments that followed.

Luke picked her up and carried her over to the bed, removing her robe before he put her down.

His own clothes followed it, until her only covering was the hard male warmth of his flesh.

Against her will, her senses responded to the proximity of him. Her body knew him now which made it all the harder. Her sensitive breasts ached for the pleasure he had given her last night, the deep inner core of her womanhood vibrantly aware of the power and sexuality of him.

When he touched her, her bones ached, even if he was only gently caressing the inner curve of her wrist as he was doing now. His marauding lips found the spot where her pulse thudded frantically against her skin and she shuddered wildly.

'Feels good, doesn't it, Gemma,' Luke whispered against her skin. 'And I can make you feel even better . . . like this . . . and this . . .'

His mouth touched the treacherous hidden pleasure spots of her body, making her cry out loud in pleasure.

'Luke!'

'Touch me,' he incited, his voice a whisper soft against her ear. 'Touch me, Gemma. Let me show you how good it can be.'

His hands guided hers over his skin until she was shaking with the wild need that filled her. She bent her head, tasting him, feeling the hard thud of his heart against his ribcage when her mouth caressed the flat button of his nipple.

'Yes . . . Yes . . . Yes, Gemma.' He breathed in harshly, expelling air from his lungs in a raw sound of pleasure as she instinctively obeyed his command. His hand slid into her nape, holding her against his body as she delicately licked and nibbled her way down it until she reached the flat plain of his belly.

'Gemma!'

Her name seemed to erupt from deep within his chest, his body shuddering, a sheen of fine sweat breaking out on his skin and tasting salt against her lips.

Her tongue-tip absorbed the tiny beads of moisture with sensual enjoyment. She had forgotten their quarrel, forgotten the harsh critical words he had flung at her.

His hand swept down over her body, cupping her breast, the texture of his palm deliciously rough against her softer skin. His thumb caressed her nipple with urgency and skill, his hands suddenly reaching beneath her armpits to lift her so that they were face to face.

'Even now, you don't know what you do to me, do you?' Luke accused hoarsely, watching the confusion darken her eyes.

What did he mean? She knew that he was aroused . . . that he wanted her.

'You want me.'

He groaned, his head tipping back, revealing the rigid muscles of his throat. His skin was dark from exposure to the sun; she wanted to reach out and place her lips to its warmth.

'I've wanted dozens of women, Gemma,' he told her brutally.

She flinched back from the cruelty of his words. Why did he have to remind her that to him she was simply one of many women who had passed through his life, or was he simply trying to reinforce the fact that all his relationships were essentially transient; that though he might want her here and now, tomorrow he might not!

She had thought that she was strong enough to endure the lack of permanency in any relationship they might have, but then she had not realised how deeply physical need could bite into the human psyche. It was like a disease from which there was no true recovery; only, if one was lucky, rare periods of remission.

'Please let me get up, Luke,' she whispered huskily. 'I ... We ... I don't want you.'

'Liar.'

The vehemence in his voice surprised her. If she was but one among many, why did he sound so bitterly determined to make her admit that she wanted him? Samantha would be more than willing to take her place, she thought acidly, and no doubt she was a far more accomplished lover than she herself could ever be.

'Luke, please let me go,' she pleaded again, unprepared for the almost savage movement of his body as it pinned hers to her bed.

'Not this time, Gemma. Not until I've imprinted myself soul deep into your consciousness. This time I'm not going to teach you how to give yourself to another man. I'm going to teach you how to give yourself to me.'

'No!' Her instinctive protest was lost beneath the

onslaught of his mouth, not violently as she had dreaded, but persuasively, tormentingly, until she was clinging eagerly to each tantalising movement of those firm lips against her own, aching for a deeper, more prolonged contact, moaning soft and low in her throat until he allowed her to capture and still his mouth's teasing movements with her own sweetly voluptuous responsiveness.

Gemma wasn't even aware of her lips parting, only of the erotic thrust of his tongue within her mouth, mirroring the aroused thrust of movement of his hips against her body.

She moaned his name against his mouth, arching eagerly against him, whimpering in a mixture of arousal and tension at the intimate contact of flesh against flesh.

His teeth took tiny bites at the swollen fullness of her mouth, his hands caressing her body.

'I want to taste very silken inch of you like this,' Luke moaned against her mouth. 'And I'm going to teach you to want to do the same to me.'

He didn't need to teach her; she was already aching to do so. Luke seemed to have released a deep vein of sexuality within her that no other man had ever come near touching.

His lips traced the line of her collarbone, and moved down over her body, feathering between her breasts and then moving with tantalising slowness over their swollen curves.

She cried out at the sensations caused by the fierce sucking movement of his mouth against her sensitive nipples, but when he stopped she ached for him to continue the erotic caress.

Already, shamingly, her body was melting in anticipation of the intimate caresses he had bestowed on it before; already she was longing to caress him with the same intimacy, eager to learn everything about him that he wanted to teach her, overwhelmed by the flood of love and desire that poured through her, obliterating all restraints.

Her hands stroked tremulously over his skin, registering with joy his reaction to her touch. Passionately she touched her mouth to the hard flatness of his stomach.

'Gemma, for God's sake . . .'

'Don't you want me to?' Her mouth trembled as she looked into his eyes and saw the fierce surge of desire darken them. This was something he didn't need to teach her, something so known and instinctive that her senses could already feel his desire for the most intimate of all caresses.

'I want to,' she whispered softly, and she saw in his eyes that she was offering him a temptation he could not resist.

Joy sang within her that she was after all able to overcome his own constraints, and as she bent her head to the taut maleness of him, she heard him cry out her name in a wild, hoarse voice edged with both delight and despair.

After that, time and reality ceased to exist. She knew that Luke lifted her and put her down on the bed, his hands and mouth caressing every pulsating inch of her body before he finally possessed her. She knew that there was a wildness, a ferocity almost, about their coming together that made it the most exquisite of pleasures; almost too exquisite to bear.

To come down from such heights, even if she was still held close to Luke's body, was too painful for stoicism and she could feel the moisture of her tears on her skin.

Luke felt them, too, his head turning and lifting, his forehand creasing in a frown, his eyes brooding and sombre as they studied her.

'Oh God, Gemma. I'm sorry ... I'm sorry.' He cradled her against his body, rocking her as though she was a child, husky words of apology filling the air.

'I didn't mean to hurt you, my darling. I didn't mean it to hurt. You just drove me beyond the limits of my control. You always have. I'm sorry, so sorry ... But I've wanted you for so long. Loved you for so long.'

He felt her tension and moved her head from his shoulder so that he could look into her eyes.

'You love me?' Gemma demanded shakily.

He grimaced bitterly. 'Didn't you guess? I don't normally go out of control in a woman's arms. Or did you think my response was the norm? Don't worry. I doubt that your polite, well-bred Tom Hardman will ever treat you like that.' His voice was bitter now, but this time with a bitterness that Gemma could recognise. Luke was jealous. Jealous of Tom.

'Well, *didn't* you guess?' he pressed tautly. 'God knows, I've made it obvious enough.

'Not to me,' Gemma told him gently. 'You see, I've been far too busy hoping that you wouldn't guess how deeply *I've* fallen in love with you to query *your* feelings.'

There was a silence that seemed to stretch for ever, when Gemma began to wonder if she had perhaps misunderstood after all, but it was too late to call back her own admission now. She closed her eyes in mute desperation, and then opened them again. Luke was staring at her.

'Just run that by me again, will you?' he demanded roughly.

'Which bit?' Although she tried to control it, her voice wobbled alarmingly.

'The bit about loving me.'

'I love you, Luke,' she told him softly. 'Perhaps in a way I always have. I know that I found that first kiss of Tom's bitterly disappointing. It was nothing like as exciting as being kissed by you. With hindsight I suspect that you spoiled me for other men,' she added ruefully. 'But you were my friend, and that was how I saw you. I was too innocent to know that friends make the very best kind of lovers.'

'Lovers?' He was frowning again, his eyes guarded.

'I ... I know how you feel about making a commitment, Luke. I do understand. I promise you that when the time comes ...'

'You'll what? Give me notice in writing that you're tired of me?'

She was so shocked that for a moment she could only stare at him. When she did speak, her voice was thready with disbelief.

'Luke, you're the one who'll get tired of me,' she protested huskily. 'That's what I was just trying to tell you. That I understand that you don't want a permanent relationship. That ...'

'You understand nothing,' he told her thickly. 'For heaven's sake, Gemma, what on earth gave you that idea? Or is it just an excuse,' he demanded tautly. 'Am I still not good enough for you?'

'*You* not good enough for *me*?' Her shock showed. 'Luke, you know I've never felt like that.'

'Don't you? Then why all this talk about us not

having a permanent relationship?'

'Not because *I* don't want one,' Gemma told him curtly. 'You're the one who doesn't want to tie himself down to one woman, or so I've heard. Everyone I meet tells me how much you like your freedom.'

'Ah.' Suddenly his face cleared, a mischievous smile tugging at the corners of his mouth. 'And shall I tell you why? Because I'm still too much in love with a girl I met when I was barely twenty years old.'

It took a while for his meaning to sink in. 'That can't be true.' Her shock showed in her voice.

'Why not? Would you prefer it not to be true?'

His expression was guarded again, and Gemma acknowledged with compassion that deep down inside Luke would always have a certain vulnerability about his past. But he need never fear that vulnerability as far as she was concerned, and she would spend the rest of her life proving it to him.

'Would you prefer me to be as sexually experienced as Samantha?' she countered.

A slow smile curled his mouth. 'No way. You can't imagine what it does to me to know that I'm the first and only man to show you the meaning of physical pleasure.'

'Oh yes, I can,' Gemma countered softly. 'I feel very much the same way, knowing that you love me . . . that you've always loved me. Tell me again, Luke. I still can't believe that I'm not dreaming.'

'Only if you promise to marry me.'

'Just as soon as it can be arranged. That way I get to keep my job, and the men's respect,' she teased him smugly.

'And that's the only reason you're marrying me?'

'Mmm ... well, there are certain other considerations.'

'Such as?'

'Such as the fact that I'm utterly and obsessively in love with you, and I want to spend the rest of my life with you.'

There was a long, satisfying pause while Luke showed her how much her feelings were reciprocated, and then he released her and settled her comfortably against his shoulder and said softly,

'You know, when I brought you out here, all I wanted was to get you into my bed. I told myself that once I had I could exorcise the past, put you out of my life for ever, but even before I touched you I knew it wasn't going to work ... that simply making love to you would only make me want you more, and not less.

'There was a moment before when I almost hated you. When I thought that you were just using me as a means of gaining sexual experience.' His mouth twisted bitterly. 'That has to have been the very worst moment of my life. I'm sorry if I ... if I hurt you when we made love,' he added gruffly.

Gemma shook her head, touching his face. 'No, you didn't hurt me.'

'But you were crying.'

'With pleasure,' she told him simply. 'I never ever thought I would experience that sort of pleasure, Luke. That was why I was crying. Even now I can hardly believe that I have.'

'If it wasn't for the fact that the steward is likely to arrive at any moment with your breakfast, I'd prove to you that you have and you can again.'

'Mmm. Do you suppose Captain Ericson can perform

marriages?' Gemma asked dreamily.

Luke grinned. 'I don't know. But the Governor can.'

In the breakfast-room, Susan Parish picked up the blue airmail letter from Gemma. She was supposed to wear glasses for reading, but vanity prevented her, and so it was several minutes before she was able to read her daughter's brief message. When she had, she read it again, her face going first pale and then unbecomingly flushed as she handed the letter to her husband and said in a tight angry voice, 'Well, if that isn't just like Gemma.'

'What's that, m'dear?'

Hugh Parish lifted his eyes briefly from *The Times* and frowned at his wife. He hated being interrupted before he had read the leader.

'Gemma's got married ... to that dreadful Luke O'Rourke. I can imagine just what everyone is going to think. If she *had* to marry the man, why couldn't she have married him here in a proper fashion, instead of in such a hole-in-the-corner way?'

'Gemma's married Luke O'Rourke?'

'Haven't I just said so, Hugh?'

To her astonishment, far from being shocked, her husband just frowned for a moment and then said, 'Oh, well, I suppose it's not as bad as it might have been. They do say that he could get a knighthood, you know. All this welfare work he does for his employees, and the man's already a millionaire.'

'Maybe so, but he isn't really our sort, Hugh. You'll have to write to Gemma.'

'What for? She's O'Rourke's responsibility now, thank God.'

He rustled the paper meaningfully to show that the subject was closed.

They were only having a week's honeymoon; that was all the time Luke could spare from the site. He had hired a villa on Antigua, set in its own grounds and completely private.

Gemma was happier than she had ever been in her life, and this was just the beginning. There were long years ahead of them to be enjoyed both as friends and lovers. They spent hours talking to one another just as they had done all those long years ago, but now the difference was that they didn't part to go to their separate beds. Now they were truly united.

She looked up as Luke crossed the small patio and deposited a cool drink beside her.

'Still love me?' he teased knowingly, bending his head to kiss her before she could reply, her lips giving him the answer to his question.

Yes, she loved him. Now and for ever, just as she knew that he loved her, and always would.

Coming Next Month

Available in April wherever paperback books are sold, or through Harlequin Reader Service:

In the U.S.
901 Fuhrmann Blvd.
P.O. Box 1397
Buffalo, N.Y. 14240-1397

In Canada
P.O. Box 603
Fort Erie, Ontario
L2A 5X3

Harlequin Regency Romance™

Romance the way it was *always* meant to be!

The time is 1811, when a Regent Prince rules the empire. The place is London, the glittering capital where rakish dukes and dazzling debutantes scheme and flirt in a dangerously exciting game. Where marriage is the passport to wealth and power, yet every girl hopes secretly for love....

Welcome to Harlequin Regency Romance where reading is an adventure and romance is *not* just a thing of the past! Two delightful books a month, beginning May '89.

Available wherever Harlequin Books are sold.

♦ Harlequin Superromance